KNOCKOUT

KNOCK OUT

K.A. HOLT

chronicle books · san francisco

To everyone who knew
there was more to the story.

Library of Congress Cataloging-in-Publication Data available.

ISBN 978-1-4521-6358-1

Manufactured in China.

Design by Jennifer Tolo Pierce.
Typeset in Glypha, Knockout, GFY Get Steve, Davy, and Lauren Brown.

10 9 8 7 6 5 4 3 2 1

Chronicle Books LLC
680 Second Street
San Francisco, California 94107

Chronicle Books—we see things differently. Become part
of our community at www.chroniclekids.com.

Who am I?
I am Levi.
I am small
but fast
I am smart
but dumb.
If you move the letters
    of my name around
you get live.
So here it is.
This is my life
This is what it's like
minute by minute
match by match
to live a Levi Life.

KNOCK

PART I

OUT ?

Mom would die,
keel over dead,
if she saw me right now.
If she saw me up here.

Got my schedule today.
First day of seventh grade
right around
the
looming
corner.
Mom wanted to come with me.
Timothy wanted to come with me.
(to get my schedule
not to seventh grade)
But I asked,
I begged
to do this myself.
Just walk the halls,
strut along,
saying Hi to friends
figuring out where my classes will be.

I can't believe they let me!
And!
I can't believe I had extra time
afterwards
to hang out in my tree.

*

The world spreads out
from the top of a tree.
I can see everything,
everyone,
and no one can see me.
I can be anything up here.

I can imagine

walking down the street,
a man with a cane,
a woman with a bike,
a kid with a bunch of friends.

I can be anyone.

I can be anything.

✱

I spy
with my
little eye
a
bird.

Not a bird in the tree
but a bird on the field—
enormous head,
big flapping wings,
running around,
crazy.

A kid in a suit
zoom
zoom
zooming.
Everyone's laughing eyes
on that beak
on those wings—

cheerleaders hoot
the coach, too,
and the bird stops
takes off his head
wings on his hips
and he's a she!

She's so funny
running around.

✶

Hello up there?
Helloooooo?

A voice I know.
A voice that makes me smile.

Only squirrels in this tree
I yell down
Only birds,
and leaves.

Leave-eyes?

Ha!
Yes!
The

LE**V**IS LE**V**IS LE**V**IS LE**V**IS
LEVIS LEVIS LEVIS LEVIS LEVIS LEVIS LEVIS LEVIS LEVIS LEVIS

see everything
you do
so YOU
better watch out.

✱

My best friend in the whole world
is a girl
I met
in kindergarten.

She is practically twice as tall as me,
she's a skinny twig, too.
If I look in the mirror
and see me,

she must look in the mirror
and see   **e**
          e
          e
          e
          e
          e
          e
          e
          e
          e.
       m

She was born early, too.
She was a two-pound baby, too.
She has an inhaler, too.
But she did not have a trach;
she does not drink high-calorie protein shakes,
and her mom doesn't make her stay home
and constantly wash her hands.

So much in common
and yet
so much apart.

*

Tam pushes her way up,
the fat branch
our bench
as she sits
and waves a piece of paper.

Show me
a wrinkle in her forehead
the only tiny sign
of her worry.

I hold my schedule
we compare
and just like that
there's no air.

*

Only one class!
Only one class together!
Tam and I have been together
every
year

since
kindergarten
and now
only
one
class!

My watch says it is precisely
definitely
thirty minutes later
than I thought.

Dang!
Timothy!
Tam and I leap from the tree,
flying squirrels

B A M

my ankles creak at the impact
but I shake
shake
shake
it off.

Wave to Tam
as she runs home,
make it to the car
—late—
look through the driver's window,
Timothy's mad.

It's not like I'm
THAT late.
It's not like I'm
a tiny baby, can't take care of himself.
It's not like I'm
going to keel over any second.
It's not like
it used to be . . .

just don't tell Timothy.
He won't believe you.

✷

You should keep better track of time.

My brother's voice is deep,
growly,
a sleepy bear waking up.

You should've let me know,
if you'll be late.
You should've known
I'd be worried.

He keeps talking.
I put in my earbuds,
turn up the Band with No Name.

Let him talk until he's blue in the face.
Talk talk talk, man.
Because my face?
It isn't blue anymore,
and it never will be.
That means
there's no reason
for him to keep nagging me.
Jeez.

✳

I don't remember
the hole in my neck,
the trach tube I needed to breathe,
the medical equipment in the house,

the almost dying,
the surgeries.
I don't remember any of it.
It's all just stories,
and it's very weird
to be the main character of a story
that's technically yours
but feels more like everyone else's.

Timothy
Timothy
Timothy says a lot
usually beginning with
You should . . .
and continuing with
blah blah blah . . .
and starting over again
until there are so many shoulds
he probably keeps a
Should Book
to keep track of his one million

TIMOTHY'S RULES FOR EVERYDAY BLAH-BLAHS

✶

It's very interesting he has so many rules
considering
he apparently broke every rule
ever made
when he was my age.

He was a legitimate delinquent!
(And he won't say what he did!)
But now,
now
I can barely sneeze
without getting the third degree
from Timothy
who thinks he is
Levi's Supreme Brother/Dad/Boss of All Things.

✶

The Band with No Name
blisters my eardrums
while Timothy grips the steering wheel
both hands
curled tight
and I wonder
what blisters Timothy's ears

when he wants to drown out the world?
Or is he too much in control
to ever want the world
to shut up?
Is Timothy's world just like the steering wheel,
and Timothy is too afraid to
loosen
his
grip?

Hand sanitizer
in the kitchen
in the car
on the shelf
never very far.
Gotta kill the germs, Levi.
Gotta stay alive, Levi.

There's a bubble trapped
in the green goo,
stuck there
trapped bits of air
in an antiseptic world.

I feel you, stuck bubble.
I feel you, trapped air.
My world keeps me close, too.

✷

Leaving the house is not exactly forbidden,
but Mom doesn't love it.
Timothy doesn't love it.
They want me safe
and healthy
and obviously
bored out of my mind.
I think they forget
being alive will not make me die.

✷

Mom and Timothy keep me close,
keep me well.
It used to be I didn't care.
It used to be that's just
How It Was.
But now . . .
now . . .

something is changing.
My insides feel like leaves
blowing blowing blowing,
a storm coming.
I want the wind to catch me
carry me off
break me free.
I don't want to be stuck inside
tangled
caught in the branches
anymore.

When I need to be alone
I sneak away,
hide in my tree.
When I'm in my tree
I can be
me.

I am short,
not tall.
I am small,
not big.

I like to mooooove
     zoom
         –d –a –s –h
                fast

I am Levi.
I am fine.
Can anyone see that?
Can anyone see me?

✶

Timothy reaches over,
pops out one of my earbuds.
Breathin' easy?

This is what Timothy and I say
instead of *Hi*
or
How are you?
or
What's up?
We've said it as long as I can remember.
I used to think everyone said it
until on the very first day of kindergarten
Tam said
Huh?

17

when I asked her: *Breathin' easy?*
And that was my first hint
that maybe my life is more

zigzagzigZagzigZagZigzigZigzag

different
than everyone else's
straight line.

✱

Breathin' easy
I answer,
popping my earbud back in.
His eyes glance from the road
to me
to the road.
He wants me to say more,
but right now
Breathin' easy is all I got.

＊

I try not to feel different
even though I'm small,
even though all vacations
are to Cincinnati
where I am knocked out
scoped
poked
X-rayed
released
like an animal caught in the wild.

I try not to feel different
even though
I am.

The good news is that I can sit in my tree
and know that Cincinnati
isn't until summer.
And even then, it's just a quick check.
They promised.

Gotta make sure my airway
is big enough
now that I could hit my growth spurt
at any second.

✷

In my room,
I look at my schedule.
It's like those To-Do lists
Mom sticks everywhere.

English
Pre-Algebra
Art
Lunch
Geography
History
P.E.

I find a pencil,
add a few more things:

Grow twelve inches
Show Dad I'm cool
Survive seventh grade

✱

Earbuds in,
the music so loud
it makes my eyes squint
my teeth snarl
my head sway
in a good way.
I feel the beat,
The Cat Tornadoes
pumping
like my own blood.
The screaming lyrics
like my own words
that I can't say.
I drown out doubts
that I will ever be anything
other than
a sick baby.
I let the noise make me whole . . .
it glues me together
gives me a voice
that is louder than my own.

✳

He'll be here soon.
Mom's mouth makes the words
I can't hear.
Earbuds out.
Get your stuff, kiddo.
He's on his way.

Dad.
I forgot.
I smile.
A Dad weekend.
A break from it all.

✳

Something happens to the air in the room
when Dad comes over.
It gets thick
gummy
trapping you
in one spot,
can't move.
Timothy goes stiff
like he's stuck in the air

and Mom goes silent
like her words are those
sanitizer bubbles
that can't escape.
Only Dad seems fine.
Hey, Sport,
he always says,
let's blow this popsicle stand.
And I fight the thick air
to get to Dad's car.

✶

I'm not sure
how Dad is my dad.
He's giant
I'm not.
He's hairy
I'm not.
He's loud
I'm not.
He's pasty white
I'm not.
But he smiles
a lot,
and I smile
a lot,

with crooked teeth
that match
proving that at least
some of his genes
are mine, too.
Plus, I like him
a lot
and so what
if Timothy
does not.

✳

Every other weekend,
four days a month.
That's all I get to see him.
Mom says it's too much.
Timothy says it's more than too much.
But I like Dad
and I miss him
and only four days a month
sucks
if you ask me
which no one does.

✷

There's this cliché about single dad apartments.
You see it in the movies,
and read it in books.
It's pretty lame
because not every grown man
is a slob
with pizza boxes
everywhere,
with piles of dirty clothes
drifting in the corners.
Every single dad doesn't live in an apartment
with barely any furniture
and mattresses on the floor.
I mean
mine does
but not every one of them does.

Just kidding.

Dad's place is actually very nice,
a house with lots of trees
and a screened-in porch

and a warm coffee smell.
(And maybe some pizza boxes
every once in a while.)
My room is comfortable,
and even Timothy has a room
if he'd ever come visit
which he has not,
not even once
that I can remember.

*

I don't know,
it's kind of fun to have a dad
who doesn't act
like a grown-up.

It's kind of fun to grab a pizza
and stay up late
and have dirty hands
and watch bad movies.

Maybe if Timothy was
more like a kid
and less like a dad

maybe now he'd be less of a
pain in my

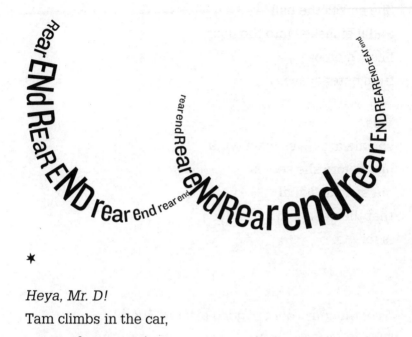

*

Heya, Mr. D!
Tam climbs in the car,
sweaty from practice.
I wrinkle my nose,
she holds her armpit in my face.

How's volleyball, Tam?

Killing it
as usual.
You guys should come to a game.
First one's next week.

Sweet!
I love watching Tam play.
She spikes the ball
and it smashes into the floor
like a meteor
from outer space.

Plus,
she always gives me a wink
just before she serves,
our special signal
that the next point
is for me.

✳

Ever thought about playing a sport, Sport?
This is what Dad asks
while he and Tam and I eat cheeseburgers
and look out over the river.

Of course I've thought about it.
But as Mom reminds me, I'm barely sixty pounds,
soaking wet.
As Mom reminds me, I'm a teacup version of
a normal human.

As Mom reminds me,
sports are dangerous
sports are for bigger kids.

I take a puff from my puffer.
Sure. I've thought about it.

Baseball?

I could throw hard
but could I throw fast?

I don't know. Seems boring.

Football?

All three of us look at each other,
laugh.

Besides, Mom won't let me do contact sports.

Why?

I point to the scar on my neck.
Duh.
I point to my lungs.
Duh.

Sport, you can do anything you want.

Yeah, Sport.
Tam winks and shoves me.

Dad puts his hand on my shoulder.
Choose something. I don't care what.
I'll pay for it.

I nod, thinking he's crazy.

We won't tell Mom.
He smiles,
looks at Tam,
holds a finger to his lips.
You get a sport.
We get a secret.

Oh, boy.
My heart does a

sKip JUMP **BEAT** skIP jump **Beat** SKIP jump bEat SKIP jump **BE** AT skip JUMP beat skip jump **Beat** SKIP jump beat skip JUMP **BEAT**

This might be a terrible idea.
But also
it might be superfun.

If being alive won't make me die
then maybe a sport won't either!

*

Only
two
more
days
of summer
and I barely remember
how to school.

*

I like school.
There. I said it.
I like it.
I like learning.
I like making people laugh.
I mean, do I like homework?
No.

Do I forget to study for tests?
All the time.
Does Mom chew her lip because
I get sick a lot?
Yep.
Does Timothy shake his head,
soooooooo disappointed?
Constantly.
But none of those things change the fact
that
I like school.
And it starts the day after tomorrow
and I can't sleep because I'm so excited,
biggest dork in the world.

✶

It's hot
bouncy
I sweat
swallow hard
will not get carsick.

Dad wants me to ride the bus
and somehow
through magic
or a miracle

or just wearing her down
convinced Mom
to let me.

And here I am
in the seat
hot
bouncing
not puking
seventh grade
awaiting me.

Man's man!
Ladies' man!
Man about town!
This is what I say on the first day.
Some people laugh,
pat me on the back.
Some people roll their eyes.

I don't really know what it means
(I saw it in a movie once)
but it's fun to say it loudly,
it's fun to be brash.

✳

Settle down, Levi.
Mr. Schoop is not a fan
of a Man's Man
Ladies' Man
Man About Town.

Well, maybe
I am not a fan
of Mr. Schoop.

✳

It's quite a trick

the

of school

balancing

wobbling

no one to catch you.

Except I have skillz . . .

I don't fall off the tightrope

I jump!

Surprise!

I *make* them laugh.

I *make* them point.

That way

the tightrope is mine

to control.

I will never be invisible

everyone will always see me.

I am too different.

I am Levi,

speck-boy,

spindle-arms,

spider-legs.

I am Levi,

baby man,

short guy.

But I will not let them

tell me what I look like.

I burn bright.
I can't be invisible
so I shine right in their eyes.

*

Hey, nerd.
Hey, turd.
Breathin' easy?
Breathin' sleepy.

Tam and I
in the halls
owning the school,
short and tall.

Bell rings
first period stings.
See you at lunch, nerd!
Only if you're lucky, turd!

*

Tam and I grab our lunch trays
but I stop short because
wait . . .
Is that a *cheerleader* at our table?

Uh
I point.
Is she like those dolphins?
The ones whose sonar gets messed up?
And they swim off?
Into the deep sea?
Away from their friends?
Confused and lost?

Oh, that's Kate!
Unlike somebody,
she shoves my arm,
we have a million classes together.
So why not lunch, too?
Tam laughs.
We plop our trays on the table across from Kate.
Why *not*?
Because lunch is practically the only time
Tam and I
have together.
But I stay quiet.

The cheerleader dolphin stares back.
She looks familiar . . .
I guess from the halls.
She smiles
slow.

For just a second
I see a shark,
but then
Tam holds up her chocolate milk.
Kate gives her a cheers with her apple juice.
And the way
Tam's smile
takes over her face
makes my own sonar
ping back something new,
something my own dolphin brain
can't quite
place.

✱

It's not a Dad night
but he's here with me.
(Mom said it was okay.)

Tam smashes the ball,
gives me so many winks
I can't keep track of the points.

We stand and cheer.

Tam finds us in the crowd,

gives me a bow.

I could never play volleyball like that

JUMP

HIT

SMASH

ATTACK

but I do love

how Tam and I are like a secret team,

winks and cheers

that only we can see.

I told Mom.

About Dad.

About him telling me to pick a sport.

I had to.

She pulls secrets from the air

like a net snatching butterflies.

She'd figure it out and be so red-faced mad.

So I told her.

She chewed her lip
said *OK.*
I said, *Wait, what?*
OK. Pick a sport.
Golf or rowing or something.
I didn't say anything.
Is golf really a sport?

✳

Clubs can be like sports, too, you know.
Teamwork, coaches, all that stuff.
You're so smart, Levi.
Have you looked at any of the clubs at school?

Clubs?
Ugh.

Like Chess Club!
You'd be great.
So smart and strategic.
You'd blow everyone away.

Sounds dorky.
Sounds dumb.

You know,
they show chess on ESPN.

I give Mom a look.
Yeah, like
ESPN
5.

Before school
I'm standing
in the lunchroom
rubbing my sleepy
eyes.

National Junior Honor Society
Model U.N.
Student Council
Math Club

So many signup sheets.
So many things
I'm not interested in.

Tam is bent over a table
signing her name.
Is it
Tall Volleyball Players Council?
Meteor Smashers Anonymous?
No.
It's Chess Club!
Huh.
Sign up, Levi!
It'll be fun!
We can hang out
and I can beat your butt.

Oh, it's ON, nerd.

Is it, turd?
'Cause I'm gonna wipe the floor with you.

Not if I wipe it with you first!

✶

I will find a sport, too,
and maybe I'll be good at it.
Maybe Mom won't catch my
secret as it flits around.
Maybe Dad will think I'm cool.

And maybe Timothy will finally see
I am me
and not some
wimpy
baby.

Karate
Gymnastics
Archery
Swimming
Diving
Soccer
Wrestling
Rowing
Tam and I sat outside for lunch
(with Kate)
and this is the list we made,
all the sports
I might like to play.

I whispered
Dad will pay, remember?

I whispered
Mom doesn't know, remember?

and would blow
her stack
or have a heart
attack
if she found out.

Tam whispered
A conspiracy

I whispered
And look at you helping me.

(Kate chattered about cheerleading
which is a sport,
she says.)

We made the list
longer and
longer and
longer
and we laughed at
so many possibilities.

✸

don't limit yourself
that's what Dad texted me.
you give yourself 2 many rules

But they aren't really my rules.

They're Mom's rules.

And Timothy's.

You can do anything you want.

Your almost a man.

Your no golfer levi.

Unless you want 2 be.

Your fierce, Sport.

Your scrappy.

You might be small

but you could kick someone's butt.

And then I wonder.

Do I want to kick someone's butt?

Hmm.

I kind of do.

I want to kick Dad's butt.

It's "YOU ' RE," Dad.

apostrophe
apostropheapostrophe
apostropheapostrophe
apostropheapostrophe
apostropheapostropheapostrophe
apostropheapostophe
Apostropheapostrophe
apostropheapostrophe
APOstrophe
apostrophe
apostrophe
apostrophe
apPOStrophe
apPOStrophe

*

I am trying to kick Tam's butt
at chess
after school
in a room
with bright lights
no windows.
It feels like detention
even though it's a club
and Mrs. Rubrick
is trying to make it fun with
cookies, sodas, classical music.
I whack Tam's queen with my rook.
Knockout! I yell,
and Tam starts to laugh.
It's called checkmate, nerd,
and you aren't even close.
She tries to teach me the rules,
but all I can think about
is the ticking of the clock
and how soon I can get
out the door.

I am not kicking anyone's butt
except for my own
for agreeing to do this.
Ugh.

✶

I take
the pieces
and make
a play.
I line up
the king
the queen
the pawns
planning a heist
to steal the knight's horse.

Tam starts to laugh
and I start to laugh
and Mrs. Rubrick
does not laugh
but the time goes by
fast.

*

Wanna come over?
Play some video games?
Tam asks me this
when Mrs. Rubrick
is finished warning us
to behave next time
or we're out of Chess Club.

OK. Let me ask.
I say
Then I'll call you.
My insides feel huge
like a balloon
is in my chest
making me float
off the ground.
I love Tam's house
though I hardly ever go because
Mom and Timothy
like to keep me at home.

*

Timothy doesn't answer
not at first
when I ask about Tam.
Then he says
Not tonight.
Maybe Tam
wants to come to our place to play?
And the balloon in my chest
bursts
and then we're home
like always.

Tam *always* comes to my house
and I barely ever go to hers.

*

(And we don't *play*.
We're *twelve years old*.
We *hang out*.
Guh.
Just more proof I am a baby
in Timothy's eyes.)

*

*Now I know what
house arrest
is like.*

Don't say that.
Timothy's eyebrows make one long line
so do his lips.

Well, it's true.
You won't let me go out.
You won't let me see Tam.
You won't let me have any fun!
Any fun!
At all!
I'm trapped here.
A prisoner.

I throw my backpack.
It slides
like a hockey puck
slamming into the wall

B O O M

goal
look at me, good at sports.

Your homework isn't done.

Your inhaler . . .

He grabs it from my backpack.

His look gets even darker.

is empty.

He throws it at my chest.

I catch it.

You're not going out.

You're not my dad!

And you should be happy about that!

✳

The Cat Tornadoes blow through me,

their music like a howling wind

tearing at my insides.

My guts spiral up

spin around and around,

my feelings . . .

confused

tangled

twisted and thrashing, but

contained for a moment.

These earbuds,
little speakers
of my soul.

In my room
I sit and breathe
try to calm down
just breathe
just breathe.
It's like I can feel cartoon smoke
moving in and out of my chest
then I realize
the mad feeling is gone
but the breathing-hard feeling is still there.
I take a puff from a new puffer,
no help.
Weird.
But then the smoky feeling goes away,
I'm breathing easy again.
No emergency jet packs to Cincinnati.
Not today.

*

I peek in Timothy's room
maybe to say I'm sorry,
maybe to tell him why
my puffer was out of juice
(I've been needing it so much)

but he isn't in there,
so I sit at his desk,
all messy,
flipping open notebooks
looking at study notes
wondering if maybe I am secretly
super extra big time smart.

We could take college classes together
and be on a TV show
about smart brothers
who are also hilarious
and good-looking.

Then, in a blue notebook, I see:

One good thing about juvie
I got to keep my journal
and when I couldn't find the words
to say out loud
I could write them down
and see them there
real
borne into this world
by my pen
and my hand
and my brain
solid feelings on the page.

Huh?

These aren't study notes.
This is a journal!
I slam it shut . . .
before I open it again.
I shouldn't read it
but I can't help it.

✳

I hear the footsteps too late.
I leap from the desk,
a surprised cat.
Timothy comes in
eyes down
backpack swinging to the floor.
He looks up,
surprised cat number two.
Levi. Hi. What are you—
My face burns.
A cat on fire.
I've lost my words.
I try to smile.
Uh, hi, Timothy.
Can I borrow your pen?

I click it
for emphasis
but before he says yes or no
I run
back to the safety of my own desk
where I rest
my forehead on the cool surface
trying so hard
to be a cool cat
who isn't killed
by its curiosity
(or its brother).

Timothy keeps a journal?
Who knew?!

Chess Club has a lot of practices
like
so
many.
They are all after school
and sometimes on Saturdays.

Chess Club is Very Serious
and Mrs. Rubrick

expects everyone to
BE RESPONSIBLE
and
NOT MISS PRACTICE.

Sometimes Chess Club
makes me sweaty
because I work so hard
coming up with strategies.

Sometimes Chess Club
makes me sunburned
because we practice outside
in the fresh air.

That's what I tell Mom.
Because Chess Club also
makes me lie.

I went to that one session
in the schoolroom
with no windows
and lights that went
bzzzzzzzzzzz
bzzzzzzzzzzz
crackle
bzzzzzzzzzzz

and Mrs. Rubrick said
we would move to the library
for the next session
and for the next session
I did move . . .
behind the school
and up my tree
using my bare feet
and knees
and I could see the whole world
and so now all my strategies
will be whispered to me
from the tops of the trees
instead of in a dingy room
with grim buzzing bees
of light.

✱

Should I feel guilty?
I ask myself this
from the tree
that is not Chess Club.

The squirrel
that is not Mrs. Rubrick
looks at me and makes a ticking noise
like
tsk, tsk, tsk, Levi.

Mom thinks
I'm at Chess Club
Mrs. Rubrick thinks
I quit.

But the clouds don't think
about me at all.
The squirrel has already
run away
and my next gambit
in this game
is to hang out,
watch the sky,
and maybe climb high
my escape
a checkmate.

✶

The giant head comes off
I squint to be sure
and yes,
yes!

It's Lunch Kate
Dolphin Kate
Shark Kate
Kate is the one inside the mascot
doing a bunch of backflips.
Kate, Tam's friend,
the sonar-challenged cheerleader.

I squint
I spy
from my roof-high
sights
and is that Tam?
In the bleachers?
Cheering Kate?
It is.

Looks like Tam's Chess Club
is branching out, too.

*

Does Tam feel guilty
for lying about Chess Club?
She doesn't know I know
she isn't there.
And she doesn't know
I'm here.
Which is weird, right?
Because that means
we're technically
lying to each other, too.

*

If I had stayed in Chess Club
would Tam have stayed there, too?
Is she out cheering on Kate
because she has nothing else to do?
I feel itchy
super itchy inside
and I don't think it's the leaves
causing it this time.

*

Timothy picks me up
in front of school.
In the car
seat belt on.
How was Chess Club?
I shrug.
You're lucky, you know.

I look out the window.
Imagine my skin
is made of four-leaf clovers.
Imagine pots of gold
shooting from the rainbows
Timothy must think
spring forth from my butt.

That you get to do this stuff.
You're a lucky kid
don't forget
that.

I mean, maybe sometimes
I feel lucky
when I'm at school

and make everyone laugh
or when I'm in my tree
and I feel like I can breathe
but there's something about having someone
look at you
with tired eyes
with

while they say you're lucky . . .
something that makes you feel
NOT so lucky,
you know?

With Timothy looking at me
I feel trapped
I feel so far from free
but I say nothing.
I watch the cars and other people.
They look like the lucky ones
not stuck in here with Timothy.

∗

I once asked Timothy
about when he was in juvie.
You know what he said?
He made his voice sound
tough,
his lips pinched together.
He stood up straight.
He barked out

MAKE
GOOD
CHOICES
DAVIDSON!

like he was in the Army or something.
Then he laughed
and hugged me out of nowhere
and whispered in my ear
If you ever go to juvie
it would be the worst
disappointment
in
my
life.

*

How could I respond to that?
Was he including Dad?
Because the way Timothy acts
around Dad,
the way his mouth tightens,
his fists clench,
the breath blows from his chest
in spurts
I can tell
Dad has disappointed Timothy
more than losing ten million dollars
in the back of a bus
and watching someone else find it
and run away with it
and never getting it back.
And it would be worse than *that*
if I went to juvie?

W H O A

*

He won't talk a lot about it.
He won't say what he did to get there.
He *does* say the clothes were scratchy,

shoes like slippers
but not soft.
He says the food wasn't as bad
as you'd think
(but Timothy eats chicken livers
on purpose
so I don't trust his opinion on food).
He says the guards weren't called guards
but they were always guarding.
He says he read
so many books
but he can't read any of the same ones again
because they make his brain
taste like juvie
whatever that means.
He won't talk about the other guys, though.
He won't talk about how they were.
Or any of his friends.
His eyes just kind of drift to the ceiling
and he bites his lip
like Mom does
when she pays bills
and then he tells me to do my homework.

*

Dad and I, in the stands
Tam is serving
I leap up
wave
holler
ready for my wink
when I see Kate
in the stands
and in a blink
she steals my wink!
Stands right up,
blocks my view
and Tam smashes the ball.

Did Tam notice
her wink was lost?
I guess not
because she goes on to score
a million more points
and I look at the scoreboard
like
What.

*

In my room
that feeling again
even with slow easy breaths
the air gets caught
stuck like a lump
at the top of my throat.

A knock.
I jump.
It's Timothy:

Can we talk?

I'm glad he can't see the lump.
I'm glad he doesn't have to know.

Sure.

*

He's going to medical school.
What!
Dr. Timothy?
What!

He's so bossy I guess that makes sense
but he's going to have to work on
his bedside manner.

Dr. Timothy wanted to tell me
before he tells Mom.
He's going to take the MCAT in a few months
and then he will pick a school
(if he passes the test)
and apply
and get loans or maybe scholarships
and go there
and never have any money
or free time again
(not like he has money
or free time now)
and then he will be a doctor
and finally finally finally
he will be able to save us all
just like he's always wanted.

(He didn't say that last part
but it's true.)

*

Mom doesn't move
like a rabbit
trying to be invisible.
She says
Medical school?
Her eyes wide wide wide.

How will we pay for it?

I'll get loans.
I'll get scholarships.
I'll figure it out.

But you have to take a test first.
To even get in.

Timothy nods again.

Then . . . you'll be gone
at school
for years.

Well, I am almost twenty-four.
Most of my friends have been gone
for a long time.

His voice is quiet.
Mom and Timothy seem to be
having two conversations
one with their mouths,
one with their eyes
so I get up
go to my room.
I feel all mixed up inside.

When Timothy's best friend, José,
joined the Army
Timothy was so sad.

He tried not to be.
He tried to be excited.
But one night I heard him
on the phone with Isa.
(Isa is his girlfriend.)

(His voice so low.
Was he crying?
I don't know.)

And I remember so clearly
he said
You left.
José is leaving.
And I'm stuck here.
House arrest
all over again.

*

I didn't ask him to stay here
and not join the Army.
I didn't ask him to stay in his room
and not save the world.
I didn't ask him to live at home
during college.
And he didn't ask *us.*
He just did it.
So he can't blame us.
We would be fine without him.
He wants to smother us
to keep us safe
which seems kind of backwards
to me.

*

It glows
like it knows my name.
Levi, it whispers.
Come here, it whispers.
Read my secrets, it whispers.
I try to ignore it
but it's like those mermaids
who lure in sailors
and make them crash boats.
I know it's stupid to get closer
but I can't stop myself.
Timothy's notebook
right there
on the kitchen counter.

This is private,
Levi.

I slam it shut
my breath in an elevator
stuck
between floors.
Slowly I open it again
the words in black ink,
messy writing.
I take Timothy's pen from my back pocket
write:

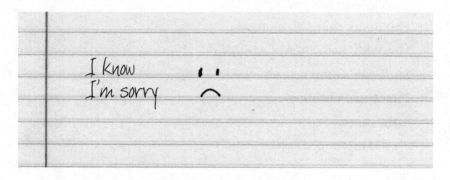

Close the notebook.
Find my breath.
(Try to.)

*

Not always,
but sometimes
I need calm in my brain.
I need lightness.
I need a different kind of air.
So I find track 9,
put it on repeat,
and let the Cat Tornadoes
lull me
before they explode . . .
Sound shards
rocking me back to my feet
again.

*

I run fast
jump on Tam's back
feet on her spine
hands on her head
she yell-laughs
leans forward
until I'm sitting on her shoulders
just like
climbing a Tam tree

and she screams
as she keeps laughing
which makes Mr. Schoop
roll his eyes
say
Cut it out, you two
and sit down.

I AM sitting down, I joke.
The whole class laughs
Mr. Schoop
snaps
his fingers
so I sit at my desk
but Tam winks
and I wink back
scoring all the points
I missed
the other night.

From the top of the tree
today
I can see
football practice.

The guys
smashing
helmets crashing.

The sharp tweet,
whistled beat,
jagged rhythm
for running feet.

I wonder what it would be like
to fly
to smash
bodies thrashing
into big piles.

How would it feel
your muscles
and bones
crushed like stones
under someone's heels?

What if
you did the crushing
the stomping
the running?
Maybe instead of small
you'd feel huge.

Maybe it's time
to pick my sport.
Maybe it's time to finally choose.

*

Kate and Tam are laughing.
Some joke
I don't know.

Have you seen *Kate, Levi?*

I'm looking at her right now.

*No, silly! I mean as the Falcon,
the mascot?*

Tam is talking fast and excited.
Kate is so crazy!
So funny!
Levi, you should see her.

That's me!
Kate says, pointing to a picture
on Tam's phone.

Craziest kid in the school.

And when Tam says that
she looks right at me
and I think
hmmm.
Is that a challenge?

Lunch is over.
Tam time over.

See you later, Levi!
Kate's voice is a singsong
like she's so super extra happy
to run off with Tam
and get rid of me.

And Tam runs off with *her.*
Does she even see me
wave good-bye?

Lunch Kate.
Cheerleader Kate.
Falcon Kate.
Crazy Kate.
She thinks she's hot stuff, huh?
Maybe I should show her what hot stuff
is really like.

✶

Because I am a secret spy
who hangs out in trees,
I know practice
by the minute.
I know no one is in the locker rooms.
I know they're all far away.
It's so easy to sneak in,
I almost feel bad.
Almost.

She'll never know it was me.
Kind of a shame, actually.
I would like some credit
for making Kate screw up her face,
for making her red-hot mad,
for making everyone laugh.

But then,
then,
as I find the falcon head
turn it upside down—
as I get out a paintbrush

I borrowed from art class
and the bottle of hot sauce
I borrowed from Mr. Schoop's desk,
and my own eyes start to water—

before I do anything at all
I wonder if maybe this is too much.
Maybe it's mean and not funny.
I don't want to hurt her
I just want to—

What's that?
In the corner?
Is it—
No—
A giant chicken head?
I laugh
and then clap my hands
over my loud mouth.

It's an old mascot costume!
Giant chicken head!
Big orange legs!
Like Big Bird, but a chicken

that might have
been run over
by a bus
457,356 years ago.

I put Kate's costume back.
I throw out the hot sauce and paintbrush.
I'm not mean,
but I am funny,
so I grab the chicken head,
I grab the legs,
and I run.

✱

The storage shed
just behind my tree
old as can be—
I throw my shoulder into the door,
bust it open
and it's perfect.
In goes the chicken head.
In go the legs.

Now
to hatch
my plan.

＊

When I asked Dad
if I could go to the football game
his eyes lit up
like I'd just grown three feet
and a six-pack.

When I told Dad
I meant by myself
to meet Tam there
(though I'm not planning to meet her
shhh)
his eyes dimmed
like I was myself again.

Please, Dad!
I don't want to be
the dorky guy
with his dad.
I want to be cool.
Please.

So he said yes.
(Dad is big on cool.)
And now I'm here at school
by myself

heading for the shed
by my tree.

*

At first I just sit
way in the back of the stands
up high
wearing my chicken head
while everyone
giggles around me.

But as the cheerleaders cheer
and Kate runs back and forth
in her falcon costume
I start my own show.

I run through the stands
mimicking her.

People hoot and laugh
as I flap my feathers
pretending I am a falcon,
pretending I am captain
of the feather-flapping team.

I make my way lower in the stands
and leap onto the field.
My heart pounds,
my face so sweaty,
and I run after Kate
who doesn't see me at first
because of her giant falcon head.

I hear a small
What?!
when she does
and I can't help but laugh
as I chase her,
a chicken run amuck.

The cheerleaders are stunned.
The crowd is cheering and laughing
as Coach Ellison
marches over to me.
But I'm too fast for her,
darting back and forth,
escaping past the fence,
and running down the road
like my head's cut off.

*

Back at the shed
to stash the legs and head
and my heart fills my whole self
my breath fills every tiny corner
of my lungs.
Oh my gosh . . .
that was fun.

*

Dad is a broken record:
Sport this, sport that,
so I snap
I could do golf!
and laugh.
Dad's face looks like I just said
I could go for a PB and mustard sandwich.

Or what about parkour?
I jump around,
leave a footprint on the wall.
Dad looks like
he's about to call
the crazy police.

Karate?
I swish my hands,
yell *HI-YA,*
but Dad just laughs:
How about not?

Well, what then?
I thought you said I could choose.

I meant choose something good, Levi,
something strong and tough.

And fun?
I add.

Well, I guess that, too.
Dad play punches my arm
and I play punch back,
dodging his soft fists,
missing his attack.

Maybe boxing
I say
just as a joke
but the way Dad's eyes light up . . .
Uh-oh.

*

Boxing!
That's it!
A knockout idea!
(Har, har)
You're so tiny,
a fly fly flyweight!
Dad laughs.
You'll be quick.
Quicker than anyone
has ever seen.
You'll sneak in jabs
so fast
you'll knock the big guys flat.

I don't know, Dad.
What if Mom finds out?
What if I get punched in the neck?

No, Levi, this is it!
Your airway is fine.
Your mom is overprotective.
One hit can't hurt you.
Plus, there's equipment.
You'll be so fine.

You'll be better than fine.
You'll be great, Sport.
This is perfect!
I'll call today.
By next week
you'll be Ali
hooking and jabbing your way
to glory.

✷

I know Dad wants this to be
our thing
a special secret
but
but
boxing?!

✷

I knock on Timothy's door.
My heart is beating fast,
but why?
Because I know he'll be mad?
Not at me
at Dad?

Because then I might be angry
that Timothy doesn't think
I can do it?

✳

He isn't in his room
and I feel that tickle
at the back of my neck.

I know it's none of my business.
I know I shouldn't look.
But Timothy's journal is right here
and it's staring at me
begging
for me to peek:

Sometimes I worry
my
brain
is
too
slow.

Sometimes I worry
this studying
this plan
it isn't quite right
after
all.

I take a pen
to leave a note
to say something like

OMG DAD WANTS ME TO DO BOXING
AND I AM FREAKING OUT

or

YOU'RE SUPER SMART
YOU'LL BE A GREAT DOCTOR
SO YOU CAN REATTACH MY HEAD
WHEN IT GETS KNOCKED OFF
AFTER TRYING OUT BOXING

but instead I write:

Your brain is fast
like a cheetah
but you better not be a cheetah
on the MCAT
or I will beat you up

I start to write
because I'm a boxer now
just so you know

but then I erase it
and leave it the way it is.
Timothy will get so mad at Dad
and I don't want him to think
he's the only one who can deal with it.

✱

You missed all the excitement
Tam says
as I plop down
my tray.

Kate stares at her burger
shooting lasers
at it.

Some crazy kid in a chicken head
ruined the game.

Ruined the game? Wow.
I take a bite of my burger.
A giant chicken?
Did it steal the ball?
Lay it like an egg?

It's not funny, Levi.
Tam is serious,
but her eyes sparkle a little.
Being the mascot is Kate's job.
She trains for it.

I don't say anything.
But maybe I smile
just a little bit.

Kate stands up,
knocking her chair back.
I have to get to class.

Oh, hey, how about that?
Now Tam and I have
some time to ourselves
to chat.

*

In my brain
I high-five
myself.

*

I'm going to start boxing
I say.
Can you believe that?
But Tam is looking out the door
where Kate walked away.

Hmm?
She doesn't even turn to look at me.

Boxing
I say again.
Hitting stuff with my fists.

She STILL isn't looking at me.

I'm going to take classes on a spaceship
and the aliens will teach me
how to level a guy with one punch
to the butt.

What?
She turns, faces me
but her eyes still seem
far away.

Nothing.

So we eat lunch
without saying another word,
both lost in our own worlds.

✳

The bell rings.
Tam says bye.
My chest feels tight.
I take a puff.
It doesn't really help.

✳

Secret parking place
after school,
Dad in the car,
sunglasses on

so silly

so

He hands me a mouth guard
some gloves
tape for my hands.
Go get 'em, tiger
he slugs my shoulder
and if the kids at the gym
hit half as hard as Dad
then I'll have to tell Mom
Chess Club is now a contact sport.

✳

Most of the time,
like eight times
out of ten,

or seven times
out of nine,
or three times
out of five,
I don't *really* mind
being small.
But sometimes
there are the cracks and crevices
between the other times
when I do mind
and I feel like I fall right through them
looking up
and I'm too tiny
to make it back to the top.

✳

Why are you all marked up?
a big guy says
while he tapes
his ham-sized
hands.

Huh?
My tape rolls
under his feet.

There
he pokes
with his loose fingertip
at my throat.

And there
he points
at my chest.

It's none of your business
I want to say
but now
there's a crowd
and they're all looking at me.

What scarred you up, kid?
someone else asks.
Probably a squirrel tried to eat him.
Confused him with some nuts
another laughs.

✳

Bear attack
I say.
Their eyes go wide.

Shark bite
Ninja fight
Sword wound

I jump on a bench,
let them see me better.

Lion scratch
Sloth bite
Pirate fight
Cactus snooze

They're laughing now.
At me?
With me?
Unclear.

Meteor smack
Alien bite
Laser fight
Demon spoon

I hop down,
finish wrapping my hands.
The guys all scatter off

shaking their heads,
still laughing.

People ask about my scars . . .

Neck slash
Rib slash

People have questions.
Well . . . I have answers.

✷

Coach shows me the ropes
quick lessons
before he leaves me to practice.

How to hit
without getting hurt.

How to breathe
when I hit.

How to dance
around the bag.

There are two guys in the ring,
a practice match.
I watch them hit each other
as I hit the bag
and I wonder,
do I want to hit someone like that?
Do I want to get hit like that?

✱

Coach calls it technique
tells me to practice
says I need it
for the ring.

So I hit the bag
over and over.

Over and over
and over and over.

And sometimes I even remember
to move my feet.

*

My gloves go in my locker.
My slobbery mouth guard
rinsed and bagged.

My fists are red
sore
my arms
also sore
but my head?

It's clear.
Like my brain can breathe
like sitting in my tree
on a cold blue sky morning.

*

So?
How'd it go?
Dad's face is so bright,
a kid on his birthday
just before ripping open so many
presents.

Fine.

That's it?
Fine?

I shrug.
I don't want to say
it was really fun.
I don't want to admit it
just yet.
I'm not ready for Dad to be right.
I want to sit with this feeling
before he takes credit.

✳

No hand sanitizer.
Don't tell Mom.
Eating dinner without washing hands.
Don't tell Mom.
Sometimes I like it better here.
Don't tell Mom.

*

I can't stop thinking
about boxing
and how boxing
makes me stop thinking.

*

When I hit the bag

BAM BAM BAM

it stopped all my thoughts
and I'm just . . . in the moment . . .

arms
fists
feet
moving
moving
an animal
not a boy
a beast
a different
me

When I hit the bag
I can finally . . . breathe.
No thinking
no worrying
just in and out
steady breath

POUND POUND POUND

The world is gone,
but also?
found.

When Dad asked what I wanted to do today
I said
Go to the park!
because Dad always gets distracted.
And today, what I itch for,
what I crave,
is to run fast
and jab jab jab . . .
practice boxing
in the hidden maze
of trees
all by myself.

The park?
Dad's face crinkled up
like I'd said
Go to the public toilet!

You mean the playground?
That's for little kids, Levi.
Why don't we go bowling
instead?

So we went bowling
and it was fun
but it wasn't like boxing.
It didn't scratch my itchy fists
that want to hit
again and again.

Hey, Levi!
Hey, man about town!
I collect my hallway high fives
and laugh
while I shoot everyone my finger guns
and shadowbox uppercuts
on my way to class.

No one's talking about the chicken head anymore.
Not even rumors.
I guess everyone's forgotten?
That was fast.

✴

I feel like it's been days
months
years
eons
since I've seen Tam
but like a glimpse
of a rare
exotic
mythical beast
there she is
out by the gym.

Tam!

Tam!

Tam!

But she doesn't see me.
Doesn't hear me.

*

Tam and Kate
Kate and Tam
Tate
Kam
look at them
just look
arm in arm
heads leaned in
supersecret fun times, I guess.
They don't need me around
when they have each other.

The Kate and Tam wall
built tall.
I can see in
but somehow
I can't
quite
break it down.

✷

Mascot tryouts,
two months away.

The flyers are everywhere.
I guess Kate will have to defend
her title.

I snatch a flyer,
stuff it in my bag.

Maybe next semester
everyone in the stands
will watch me
instead of her.
Maybe Tam will call *me* craziest
instead of her.

✷

There it is again
on the counter.
I should leave it be
but I want to see
if Timothy
wrote back to me.

WHY IS THIS NOTEBOOK
ON THE KITCHEN COUNTER
IN MY WAY
AND GETTING SPLASHED
WITH SINK WATER?
CAN SOMEONE PUT IT AWAY, PLEASE?

Ha!

That's *Mom's* handwriting.

Hi, Mom!

*

Talk to me, Levi.
Tell me about . . . things.
Mom plops on the couch,
her head snuggles my shoulder.

We could talk about Dad.
We could talk about Tam.
We could talk about Timothy.
Or . . . we could just . . . be.

I have a joke, I offer.
Her hair smells like outside
and fajitas
and shampoo.

Okay, she says. *Shoot.*

What's brown and sticky?
I pause for dramatic effect.

I don't know. What?

A stick.
Timothy slides in next to us,
stealing my punchline,

his big body making the couch sag
into a smile.

That's a terrible joke
Mom laughs.
And we all sit together
trying to out-bad-joke each other
laughing and laughing
until the oven dings
and it's time to eat.

✳

At dinner it happens.
My head gets light
the air
it seems stuck
like trying to suck
glue through a straw.
Breathin' easy, Levi?
Timothy sees it first.
I nod.
I want to be OK.
But the air can't find a way
into my lungs.
Get his inhaler.
Mom says this to Timothy

as if I weren't right here,
as if I couldn't stand up and find it
myself.

They are in Sick Levi Mode,
three seconds flat.

Timothy has my puffer,
is down on his knees
beside me,
dinner forgotten.

Should I get the Os?
I take two puffs.
I take two more.
The air flows better
but still not great.

No oxygen
I say.
But really
I have no say.

Mom has her purse already.
Off to the ER we go.

✷

Oxygen
Steroids
Nebulizer

Oxygen
Steroids
Nebulizer

By the time I can breathe again
my heart rate is one million
my head is full of bees
my hands are shaking
my palms damp
my face sweaty
but the air sings in my lungs
fills every tiny crevice
and I feel like a balloon
like I might float to the ceiling
stay there a while.

The doctor says it's just a bad cold.
She says we can go home.
No supersonic jets to Cincinnati
today.

*

Mom seems relieved.
Timothy does, too.
But do either of them think
we could have just fixed me up
at home
instead?
We have everything we need
and maybe they could trust me
to say how I'm feeling
without always packing up
and running
to the hospital.

*

Home sick today.
No school.
It's a couch potato
nebulizer
puffer
kind of day.

Timothy stayed home.
No class for him
either.

*

One of my earliest memories . . .
I was feeling kind of sick
and Timothy
brought me my Spaceship Blanket,
tucked it around me
made me feel safe.

So when he finds it today
and tucks it under my cheek
I have this deep deep feeling
of calm.
And even though Spaceship Blanket
is a baby blanket
for once, I don't feel like a baby
at all.

*

What's that?
He points to the right
and I turn to look
while he grabs my wrist
puts a stethoscope over my shirt.

Is that a pterodactyl?
A dragon?
A princess?

This little game of distraction
is silly now
but I can't remember a time
when we haven't played it.

I see an angry burrito.
I see a turtle car.
I see galaxies swirl.

The stethoscope is as old
as me
and over the years
Timothy's gotten as good
as a doctor
in hearing weird things
crackling up
from my lungs.

I see a spaceship.
I see a knight
who talks with his hands.

Timothy distracts me
making sure I'm still breathing easy,
making sure the oxygen tanks
can stay
in the closet.

It's like he's a doctor
already . . .
Like Dr. Sawyer
but with more
hair.

✱

I ate soup.
He ate some, too.
We watched bad TV.
(ESPN 5!)
(No chess.)

We talked about school.
I told him
about Tam and Kate
(but not about boxing)
(and not about the chicken head)

but I did
mention
maybe doing
mascot tryouts.

He laughed,
said that sounded fun.
He listened,
he told me about Isa calling.
He told me about José
in Afghanistan
still.

We talked more
and ate more soup.
And I wonder
why does Timothy
only seem to know me
really (or take time to know me?)
when I'm not breathing easy?

✸

Breathin' easy?
Tam pops through my window
plops on the floor

grabs a pillow
props up her head.

Does your mom know you're here?
Sneaking into a boy's room?

We both make horror show faces
and laugh.

Just heading home from the game.
No chicken tonight.
So Kate was happy.

I try not to frown.
Five seconds in and already
Kate
is somehow here, too.
Isn't there anywhere
she isn't?

Did we win?

I don't even know!
She laughs again.
Feeling better?

Yeah, but Mom thinks I'm dying.

Again?

I half-smile.
She half-smiles back.
You're like a zombie, Levi,
all that almost dying and coming back.

Zombies have to actually die
and then come back.

You did that, too.

Shut up.

She hands me a candy bar
two bites missing.
You look alive to me.
No zombies here.

I take a double shot from my inhaler
shrug.
I feel at least one-quarter human,
three-quarters zombie.

Well, I'll take it.
She stares at the ceiling.

I stare at the ceiling.
And I try my best
to actually breathe easy.

＊

I have so much to tell Tam that
I can't find the words
to say anything.

＊

This morning
my alarm
my blanket pulled over
my head
my eyes
won't open
too early
too early
but school
but school
always school
sit up
look out the window
face the day
and I see it
on my desk

Timothy's notebook
weird.
Mom must have messed up,
given it to me instead of him.
I should return it.
I shouldn't open it.
But the mermaids sing
and there I am
in my pajamas
Timothy's notebook on my lap
open.
How did that happen?

A personal journal is very crowded
with so many eyes ⌣ •

Timothy wrote that
under my *Hi, Mom!*

A page is folded down.
It wasn't folded before.

When I was his age I was such a mess
stumbling through life
every minute
a paper cut
every second
a painful slice
of life.

Could he understand it?
If I told him?
Could he understand
without feeling like it was his fault?

It wasn't his fault.
It never was.
It was just life.
(And Dad's fault.)
(Is it fair for me to say that?)
(Yes, I think it is.)

As if the mermaids want me to say something,
I grab Timothy's pen from my desk
and I write:

> What do you mean?
> Paper cuts?
> What do you mean?
> Painful?
> Every day was like that for you?
> But, why?

I slide the journal under his door
just before
I leave for the bus.

✳

Feeling better?
Dad asks this
when I get into the car
toss my backpack
on the floor.
I nod.
Think you're up for some boxing?
I shrug.

I'm TOTALLY up for boxing.
Totally up for feeling the beat
in my feet.
Totally up for dancing
with my fists.
But I still feel weird about telling Dad.
For some reason
this "who discovered boxing first" fight
is a fight I want to win.

What's Timothy up to these days?
He sneaks that one in.

I could say
Studying for doctor school.
I could say
Driving me crazy.
I could say
Making sure I do my homework,
leaving me his journal,
keeping me breathing easy.

But I just shrug.
I figure Dad can ask Timothy.
I'm no informant,
I'm no spy.

He'll have to break down the wall
or climb over it
to catch Timothy's eye.

✻

I see the dudes laughing
huddled up
watching me
not even pretending not to.

It's not like I don't know
my arms are skinny
my legs are skinnier.

It's not like I don't know
my head is

hugehugehugehugehugehugehuge
hugehugehugehugehugehugehuge
HUGEHUGEhugehugehuge
hugehugehuge hugehugehuge
hugehugehuge hugehugehuge
hugehugehuge HUGEHUGE
HUGEHUGE H U HUGEHUGE
HUGEHUGE Ge HUGEHUGE
HUGEHUGE hugehugehugehuge HUGEHUGE
HUGEHUGEHUGEHUGEHUGE

my chest so thin
you can count all the ribs.

It doesn't mean I don't try hard.
It doesn't mean I don't hit harder
like my muscles
are huge and dangerous
able to kill turds like those guys
with a single hit.

So I just punch the bag

hard

harder

hardest

and pretend I don't see.

*

The bag is every dude here
the bag is Dad
the bag is Kate
the bag is Timothy
the bag is Tam
the bag is me

✷

Bet you fifty bucks
you can't hit my face
says a boxing guy
with a nose the size of Cleveland.

He smiles at the others
and I just sigh.
Have these guys
seen any movies,
ever?
Can't they see how clichéd they are?
Jeez.

I try to walk away
but the guy jumps in front of me
points to his nose
Fifty—
but he doesn't finish
because I surprise him

WHAM

right into the slant
of his giant schnoz.

Blood explodes
the guys all yell
WHOA
and *HOLY #$%^^*!, BRO*
and the guy staggers back
dripping surprise.

I wasn't wearing a glove
my fingers hurt
but I don't want it to show.

You said fifty bucks
I shake my fist
but my voice is strong.

The guy goes to his locker
pulls out a bill
wads it up
throws it at me
I catch it
smile.

*

How was practice?

Fine.
I think of the hit
of the money in my pocket.
Great, actually.
And I smile.
In fact,
Dad,
I was wondering . . .
can I go to more practices?
Maybe a couple of times a week?

Dad bites his lip
looks at me
then back at the road.

Don't think I can afford that, kiddo.
It's not like you're trying out for the Olympic team
or something.
But I'm glad you're having fun!

Wait.
What?

But Dad.
You wanted me to do this.
You want me to box,
to be a man,
to be the fly-fly-flyweight
champion of the world.

I don't have the cash, Levi.
I am low on moola, benjamins, smackers.

But.
But.
I can't think of a response.
He wanted me to do this.
And now I want to do this.

He's created this monster
and he doesn't want to feed it?

*

Its blue cover
familiar now
I don't even care that
it isn't mine.
I sit at his desk
and I use his pen,
the one I stole:

Why do I feel two things at once?
like when I think Dad's ok
and I also think he's not

I close it.
Leave it on his desk.

*

Find a sport, Sport!
Be more sporty, Sport!
Oh, you found a sport, Sport?
Good job, Sport!
Wait, your sport costs money?
Well, sorry, Sport.
I wanted to encourage you, Sport,
but I didn't think you'd actually do it,
Sport.

So.

Here I am
in the leaves
of my tree
mind churning
fists clenching
breathing
thinking
breathing
thinking

and then it comes to me
and I climb out of my tree.
He made me start boxing
now let's see him stop me.

★

Hey, Levi.

Hey, Coach.

Whatcha doing here?

Uh . . . boxing, silly.

*Yeah, well, your dad
only signed you up
for two classes a month.*

It's OK. I'll stay. He'll pay.

Side-eye.

*No, really,
it's fine.*

*All right, then,
get in there.*

I smile.
Dad won't mind
right?
By the time he finds out
I've added extra practices
he'll be superproud
that I love to fight.
Right?

*

See, you need to guess:
What
is
he
thinking?

Coach points at the kid in the ring
across from me.

Get in his head.
Trick him with your moves.
But don't let him trick you
with his.

I nod
bite hard
on my mouth guard.

And then

We dance

back and forth
to and fro
our feet hopping
sliding
to music only
we can hear.

The beat
beat
beat.

The drum
drum
drum.

The hum
hum
hum
of two heartbeats
becoming one.

*

My fist connects.
His does, too.
Pain explodes
in fireworks
in sparkles
in blazes
I suck in
deep breaths
more energy
to ignite

fireworksfireworksfireworksfireworks
fireworksfireworksfireworksfireworksfireworks
fireworksfireworksfireworksfireworksfireworks

for him
sparkles in his nose
blazes setting fire
to his raw flank.

*

I move from minute to minute,
hour to hour,
a hop skip jump
from one second
to the next,
and my earbuds scream
The Band With No Name,
a soundtrack
moving me along,
giving me big beats
like ellipses . . .
connecting me to the moments
strewn about my days.

*

Cheerleader practice.
Mascot practice.
If I walk to the boxing gym
I get to watch everything
as I go past.

It's different than in my tree
watching tiny people
scatter around.

From up close I see the routines
hear Coach Ellison
see Kate
and how hard she works.

Tips and tricks for me
and the chicken head.

It's nice to get my blood pumping
before I get to the gym,
and also it's nice
to spy
on everything
else.

✴

(It's also nice
to not ask Dad for a ride
so that way
he doesn't know
just how many visits to the gym
he's sponsored
in the past few days.)

*

My glove connects
because he did not jab.
Yep.
I guessed right.

His head whips to the side
and I close in
because right now
I know
he isn't thinking about his next hit,
he's thinking about *MY* next hit
so I give it to him
and he's back against the ropes
and Coach is yelling
Wow! Levi!
Good job!
Nice moves!
But his words are a blur
because my fists
my feet
are a symphony
and I am

Turning
Up
The
Volume.

*

Under my door
a familiar blue
says hello.

> Tell me what happened.
> What did he say?
> What did he do?
> I can try to fix it,
> if you want me to.

I can't tell him what happened,
I don't need him to fix it.
I've already fixed it.
All by myself.

I put on the chicken head
and boy is it hot
so hot
oven hot
baking hot
sweating
sweltering
Fried Levi.
But I don't care
because in this head
in this suit
I get to be huge
bigger than anything
all eyes on me.

*

Kate is looking for me this time,
her falcon head swivels, slow motion
her wing points at me
as I run

fly
down the stairs in the stands,
as I leap onto the field.
She squawks
flaps,
I squawk
flap
hop
leap
The crowd . . .
the crowd!
They're on their feet
laughing and cheering.

Kate runs at me.
I dodge her
(thanks, boxing!).
Coach Ellison is after me now,
she squawks loud, too,
as I zigzag free
along the sidelines
players slapping my shoulders,
laughing so hard
coaches steamed, yelling.

I stop.
In one glorious moment
drop my pants
show the stands
the full moon
is mine
tonight.

And then I'm gone.
Chicken head lost to the wind.
And as I laugh hard
I hear the cheering
all the way
from the shed.

✱

There's still plenty of time
until mascot tryouts.
Plenty of time
teasing Kate on the field.
Plenty of time
before my audition kills
and everyone sees it's me . . .
the big reveal!

Kids come up to Kate
all through lunch
they think she's in on it,
that she and the chicken head
have created a skit.
Her mouth is tight.
She doesn't say anything.
But I'm smiling.
And Tam and I talk about
dumb things
fun things
and it's almost like Kate
isn't there
at all.

I'm really good.
No, I don't think we have time
for a whole game.
I need to rest my brain.
But
some day.
I will smoke you, Mom.

You'll see all my trickiest chess moves.
Just not today.
Is that OK?
No, it's not too much.
Practice makes perfect, right?

Same goes for lying.

Just breathe, Levi.
Stay cool.
Stay cool.
Mom will never guess
not in a million years
you're boxing
instead of
playing chess.

✳

Dad called the house
which he never does.
He's yelling
but I can't talk.
Mom'll hear everything.

This bill!
Levi!
My god!
What have you—
I can't even—

I guess going to boxing
more than twice a month
costs a lot more
than I thought.

Mom is staring
Timothy is staring
I just swallow
say nothing
hope they can't hear the yelling

about all the money he's spent
and how next week he is
personally
walking
me
in
and talking
to the
coach.

I say, *OK.*
I say, *See you then.*
Hang up the phone
so fast
you might think
it was on fire.

✳

What was that all about?
Look who suddenly appears!
Look who's all ears!
The mystery brother, formerly known as Timothy.
What did he want?

I deflect Timothy's questions
just like we're boxing.
Even more practice
for becoming the
fly-fly-flyweight
champion of the world.

✳

Timothy's journal is on my desk.
Again.
I open it.
Again.

What's going on, Levi?
You seem a little . . .
off.
Do you want to talk about Dad,
and whatever's going
on?

You can talk about your feelings, Levi.
You know I'll listen, don't you?
Even if I'm not always physically here
I'm always here for you.

What do I say
to something like that?
I know he'll listen,
just . . .
what is it called
when you want to talk
but your feelings are all jumbled

and you don't know what to say?

Aargh.

What even *IS* that?

I write:

> I have feelings
> just like you
> I'm figuring things out
> just like you
> but also

And this part, I write

then erase

then write again:

> I miss you.

*

Get in the car.
Little beard hairs shake.
Dad is so mad.

I'm glad you like boxing, Levi,
but, Sport,
I said no to more practices
I said no.

I look at the floor.

There's no money for this.
You'll have to work it off.
You better think of a plan.
You're going to have to talk to Coach.

*

Levi!
Coach's face breaks out
into a big fat smile
C'mon, killer, let's see what you've got.

And we shadowbox
around the lobby.
I'm fast.
So fast.
Practice makes
perfect.

It only takes a second
for me to forget
Dad is even there.
But he sucks in his breath,
loud.

I don't know
if he's ever
looked at me like that,
his eyes
wide
his hand strokes his beard
like he is some supersmart
actual lumberjack
and he says
Jeez, Levi
Am I gonna have to take out a second mortgage?

Coach goes up to him
I hear *money, tight*
I hear *working, gym*
I hear *towels, wash*
I hear *hate to lose him*
I hear *talented*

They shake hands
both look at me
and now I'm Coach's servant, I guess
but I don't care.

Bye, Dad!
I wave as I run to the locker room
and Dad's face
his face
I wish I had a picture
of that proud
mouth
in a wide open
O
(And I try not to think about
how he wanted me to do this
but how surprised he is
I've actually done it.)

*

If you lived in a tent
under someone's armpit
that would be
a one hundred percent accurate match
for this locker room.

Hey, Davidson, you're back.
The huge kid looms over me.
Ready for a match?

I smile
chew my mouth guard
look him up and down.
I don't know
I say,
wrapping my hands.
I wouldn't want you to get hurt.

The guys all laugh,
but I'm not kidding.

*

Here's the thing about boxing:

I thought it would be all about smashing noses
and being smashed.

But boxing is not that
at all.

It's about feeling your world
tighten into a pinprick
of just you
and your opponent.

It's about quick feet,
and quicker thinking.

It's like chess,
but with your body.

All movement.
Strategy.

It sounds weird to say this,
but
with boxing?
There is, like,
beauty.

Coach steps between us,
ends the sparring,
one hand on my sweaty shoulder
the other on my opponent's.
Nice fight.
He nods.

You're a little beast, Davidson.
My opponent smiles,
takes off his headgear,
shakes his sweat in my face.

Gross.
But I laugh
because that guy?
He's like ten times sweatier than I am.

I could do this all day.

✷

Let's play.
First time I've seen Timothy
in days.
He has a chessboard in a box
under his arm.

No thanks.

He looks surprised.

It's just,
I say
walking backwards toward my room,
my eyes
they're fried
so tired.
I think I'll rest.

He looks confused.

Even though I want to hang out.
Even though I miss him,
I'm terrible at chess.

He'd know in a heartbeat
if we started a game.
He'd know in a flash
Chess Club is fake.

*

Another Friday night.
This time I tell Mom
I have a chess match.

Oh! Levi! Exciting!
Can I come watch?

I'll be too nervous.
Maybe next time?

Where is it?
I'll drive you.

It's at school.
I can walk.

Don't be silly, Levi.
Get in the car.

So now we're driving
to my fake chess match
on the dark side of the school,
instead of me running
towards the Friday night lights
where my chicken head
is waiting for me.

*

You're sure it's tonight?
Mom squints.
Looks pretty dark.

I'll be fine!
Thanks for the ride!

I hop out of the car and run.
The shadows hide me
while her car idles.
She won't leave
until she knows I'm safe.

It's OK!
I swear!
The chess room is right down there.

I point to a window
with one light on.
Mom seems suspicious
but she nods,
drives away.

And then I run
all the way to the shed
to find my head
so I can get to the game.

Through the chicken head
I see Tam in the stands
right by the sidelines
cheering Kate,
sitting with people
I don't know.

I run to them
grab a kid's popcorn
throw a kernel in the air
catch it in my beak
make everyone laugh
(except for the kid
and Tam).

Then I fling myself
to the field.
Kate rips off her falcon head
starts to yell.
I mimic her moves
(but keep the chicken head on)
bigger,
sillier,
the crowd goes wild.

Except for Tam,
she's on her feet,
her hands on her hips.
She's not laughing.

I flap my arms and get off the field.
Coach Ellison didn't chase me.
I didn't even see her
weird.

I'm sweating
when I get to the old shed.
I toss in the head
toss in the legs
take two puffs

feel my lungs clear
that's when I hear the cough
but it's not mine for once.
It's from the back.
It's from the dark.

I turn to run,
but it's too late.
Coach Ellison steps out of the shadows,
arms crossed tight.
I'm breathing enough air for ten people
but I can't stop opening and closing my mouth
I need a word puffer
because my sounds are all lost.

Put that back where it belongs.
No more chicken head, Levi.
You're done.

No sound comes out
my mouth
gasping for words.

Coach Ellison walks past
turns around
I guess I'll be seeing you
in the principal's office Monday?

★

The phone rings
very early
Monday morning.

I leap up
trip out of bed
stumble fast
into the hall
try to
beat Mom—

Mom: *Hello?*
Yes, this is she.
Hmm?
What?!

Her eyes turn to me
wide
then
slits

Oh really.
Oh REALLY.
Yes, I will be there.
Thank you for calling.

The phone goes click
back in its base.
Mom turns to me,
red crawls into her cheeks
anger crawls into her words

Get dressed, you.
Now.

And that quiet voice,
it's the one saved for mean doctors
and insurance companies on the phone
not
usually
for
me.

Uh-oh.

Driving to school
Mom keeps looking at me.
Finally
I say
What?

Half her mouth smiles.
You stole a chicken costume.
Really?

I nod,
my mouth opens
happiness flies out of me
as I describe
running in the stands
making everyone laugh
being crazy
being alive.

Mom's eyes on the road,
her voice soft now
I would've never dared to think,
Levi,
you'd be so big now.
I would've never dared to dream.

Her hand shoots out
grabs my knee
gives it a squeeze.

You're still in trouble
she says,
pointing at me now.

But wow, Levi.
Just . . . look at you.
Wow.

One million detentions.
Basically
every day
after school
helping Coach Ellison
doing whatever she says.
Mom isn't happy.
Principal McGee isn't happy.
I am not happy.
And now I have to apologize
to Kate
and the whole
entire
school.

My face burns
my chest is tight
I hold the microphone
look at the speaker in the wall
where my voice will carry through

the halls
try to break it
with my brain.

Hi, everyone.
My voice cracks.
I clear my throat.
This is Levi Davidson.
I want to say I'm sorry
I borrowed the chicken head
and disrupted the cheerleaders
and I'm sorry to Kate, the true Falcon,
for everything.
I apologize.

Thank you, Levi.
Principal McGee is very serious.
She looks me up and down.
It's one thing to be a class clown
and it's another to be mean and disruptive.
Do you think you can tell the difference now?
She says this into the mic
I could not
be more
embarrassed.

I nod.

She points to the mic,
I squeak out
Yes.

She nods and clicks off the mic.

Coach Ellison and I have agreed,
along with the detentions,
you may not
try out for
mascot
this year.

What!

✳

Not allowed!

To try out!

For mascot!

AAAAARRGHHH!

✶

Most kids laugh
slap my back
when I walk down the hall.

They
shake their heads
seem impressed
can't believe I did it
Man's man! Ladies' man! Chicken man! Ha!

But Tam.
Tam.
Tam is not impressed.
Tam is not smiling.
Or laughing.

Hey, nerd, I say, trying to smile.
Turd, she mutters,
then says nothing at all.

✶

OW.
The shock throws me back
two steps at least.

Bright white light
explodes
in my
right eye.
Kate looks almost as surprised
as I feel.
What the heck, Kate?!
The sting on my face
burns
like she's left behind some of her hand
and I'm allergic to it.

She and Tam walk away
with no words
just a pink handprint
saying everything
for them.

Tam—
I call after them,
I was just joking around!
Plus, I said I was sorry!

But she doesn't hear
because she's already down the hall
earbuds smashed in her ears.

✱

Come on!
The words out before I feel them.
I only hear them.
Come on!
I swear at the boys staring.
I hit my chest with both gloves
a gorilla
marking territory.
Come on!
I scream it through my mouth guard.

Why am I so mad?
Because I got caught?
Because Kate hit me?
Because Tam won't talk?
Because I never see Timothy?
Because I'm not the son Dad wants?

Come on!
Come on!
Come on!

So one of the guys, smirking,
climbs in the ring, and
before his feet are set

he's on his butt
my hook landing square under his jaw.
But he's up
dancing now
eyes serious now.

Come on!
I hit my chest again.
He swings
he's fast
but I'm faster
I duck
I dart
I spin
I land three more punches,
he staggers back.
No one's laughing now.
Coach by the doorway
watching close.
We're dancing,
this guy and me.
He can't land one hit.
I am too fast
a tiny gorilla,
mad,
smart,

and now I'm laughing
and Coach steps into the ring.
Enough
he says.
Enough.
But I feel like finally
finally
I'm just getting started.

✳

The kid takes a swing.
This one lands
right in my chest.
I gasp,
feel something caving in.
He hits me again
and I'm on my knees.

Enough, I said!
Coach yells
pulls me to my feet.
I step out of the ring
and things
go a little sideways.
My ears start to ring
as I fall

lights out
knocked out
smashing my head
into the concrete wall.

✳

Bright
           lights
head
           hurts
head
           hurts
head
           hurts
head
           hurts
head
           hurts
HEAD
           HURTS
where am I?

✳

What were you DOING?
Mom's hands on my face
her eyes so big

but squinting
confused.

Why were you BOXING?
Not at Chess Club?
Mrs. Rubrick said
you've only been to Chess Club
once
all year?!
Levi.
First the mascot thing
and now this?!
What were you DOING?
WHO ARE YOU?

Mom looks at me
like she looks at Dad
when he says something and her brain
just
can't
compute.

My mouth is so dry,
my head so aching,
I am afraid to say
anything

because I don't want

to feel like
my brain.

Timothy stands in the doorway
of my hospital room.
looking
looking
looking
at me.

I'm pretending to be
asleep.

He doesn't move
just leans against
the door

like he isn't sure
he's in the right room.

Mom is asleep
her head
on my bed,
her back bent,
her sleeping body
angles in a chair.

Timothy sees I'm awake.
I see his Adam's apple
go up
then down.
He walks over
tucks Spaceship Blanket under my head
then turns
without a word
and walks away.

Dad is here now.
No one else.
He looks so weird
pale
hand on his beard

hand in his pocket
hand on his beard again.
The room seems smaller
with him standing here.
I don't really like hospitals
he says
and Duh
who the heck does?

Mom and Timothy went to go get food,
so,
uh,
I'll just sit here with you.
Cool?

Dad is watching me.

I pretend
I'm not watching him
watch me.

He pretends
he doesn't see me
watching him
watch me.

✱

Then.

✱

This old thing?
Dad sees Spaceship Blanket
tucked under me.
He laughs,
tries to take it.
I pull it back,
feel my face go slack.
Why would he laugh?

Doesn't your mom know
you don't need that?
You're a boxer!
Seventh grade!
I can take it.
Give it here.
Dad reaches,
I pull away,
stuff Spaceship Blanket
in between
the bed
and my back.

Boxers don't need baby blankets.
Come on!
He smiles, laughs, reaches out again
like it's just a silly joke.

I jump up
even though my head spins,
take Spaceship Blanket
and my IV pole,
making sure to slam
the bathroom door
hard.

K N O C K
K N O C K
K N O C K

My cheeks burn.
He thinks I'm a baby.
Tiny baby Levi
Needs his blankie to sleep.

How about you just zip it?
I shout through the door.
Comb your beard
over your mouth
or something?

Jeez, relax.
Keep the blanket, Levi.
I was kidding
mostly.

✶

My guts are spinning.

Boxing
Chicken head
I feel it all
crumble away
because
he's right
I *am* a baby.
One big punch
one fall
and here I am
a helpless little kid
who can't do anything.

And then a thought like a worm
slithers into my pounding head.
Is *that* why Tam
likes Kate instead?

You did this to him!
Mom shouts it
like we are on some reality TV show.

Dad shakes his head.
She grabs his arm
drags him
out of the room.

In and out.
Dreams and blackness.
Blurry walls
blurry sounds
in and out
day by day
or maybe it hasn't been that long?
Everything is upside down.
I don't really remember
getting smashed in the head.
They say I stumbled forward,
my head glanced the wall.
Just a glance
but enough

to knock me down
and out.

A boxing match
with a wall . . .
Can't train
for that.

Trust can't really be explained
because it's a feeling
like love.
But it's kind of more than that
because trust has long arms
and an open face
and it believes the words
you say.

Love can't be lost
when it comes to moms
but trust can
curl back its arms
close off its face
and disappear
a puff of smoke
a memory

nothing left for you to hold on to.
Nothing left for you to do.

★

You lied to me.
Mom says this as she holds up a cup,
puts the straw in my mouth
as if my hands
have concussions, too.

These *were your chess moves?*
Your strategies against me?
Lies upon lies?
Levi!
Look at me!

I'm sorry.

My words slip around the straw.
And I can't find any more of them
because I'm sorry I lied
but I'm not sorry I did any of this.
I like being fast
I like keeping guys on the move
in the ring
and at school
fists or wits.

I like all of it
all of it
and Mom doesn't understand
and I don't have the words
to make her get how
all of this stuff makes me ME
and not the tiny baby
she took care of
way back when.

All trust has been lost, Levi.
Her words settle in my chest
like they are a ball of dust

and I can't swallow the fact that
my choices seem to be:
Keep Mom's trust or
keep being me.

✱

How many doctors can you fit in one room?
This is crazy.
Am I dying?
My heart starts to beat fast
the monitor snitches on me
with its beepbeepbeepbeeps.

When I cracked my head
I must have really knocked something loose.
I don't feel bad, though
just sore
and dumb
and sad.

One doctor flips open a laptop,
clicks on some X-rays.
Another clears her throat.
Mom holds my hand.
I don't like this.
I don't like it at all.

✳

With Levi's history,
we gave him a full upper body scan,
the doctor says.

His concussion will heal
but there are other
nonrelated
areas of concern.

Mom's face goes white.

I'm not overly *concerned,*
the doctor says, holding up her hand,
I just want to err on the side of caution.

She points to pictures
of my lungs
blown up huge.

She taps a couple of buttons
and my throat
takes my lungs' place
on the screen.

And again
Considering his history
it looks okay.
Except for here
and
here
and
here.
When did you say you were going back?
To Cincinnati, I mean?

This summer
Mom and I say
at the same time.

Maybe think about going sooner
the doctor says.
Don't panic, but go sooner.

Her smile says
I AM NICE
BUT I AM WORRIED.

So it wasn't just me
whacking my head?
This is something different
wrong with me?

Not wrong, exactly,
the doctor says,
just needing to be further explored.

Further explored.
Like I am an unknown land.
A lost planet.

Have you been having trouble breathing, Levi?
She looks at my chart.
I see you've been using your inhaler . . .
a lot.

I nod.

Too much activity
Mom says.
This mascot thing.
Boxing.
Too much, Levi.
It's too much.

No!
I shout.
This was all happening
way before that!

Then I realize what I've said.
What I just admitted.
Yet another secret
I've been keeping from her,
and ...

Mom's face.
Mom's face.
Mom's face.

Go ahead and get it checked out, OK?
the doctor interrupts.

And since you have a team
in Cincinnati . . .
they should probably take it from here.

✱

I'll give them a call as soon as we get home.
Mom gives me a look
but squeezes my knee
and I feel all the anger leave the room.
I wish my breath would fill it up instead.
Why
why
why
is this kind of thing
always happening?

I hate all this.
I hate it so much.
Why can't I be Timothy?
Why can't I be Kate?
Why can't I be
that guy I punched?
A regular kid doing regular things?

Why am I small
and always wrong?
Why is something always broken
and never the way it should be?

✳

Is Timothy here?
or not here?
I sleep
and I wake
but sometimes the two
are confused.
Did I hear him say
it's his fault
or did I dream that?
Did he say he hasn't been around
or did I make that up?
Is he sad?
Or mad?
I can't tell what's real
what's a dream.
Is Timothy here at all?
Or is he still
just studying?

*

I know one thing that's real.
Tam hasn't come to visit.
Not once.
Not even in a dream
or a fake dream
or anything.

*

Mom
of course
is here.
Mom is always here.
Also always here now?
Something burning
in my chest
a red-hot ball
of feelings
trying to get out
and the more Timothy is not here
the more Dad is not here
the more Tam is not here
the redder
and hotter
my burning chest
gets.

*

A blue notebook
on my hospital side table.
My head is still swimmy
but that doesn't mean I can't write:

> I never see you
> a ghost
> a wisp of air
> a smell in the kitchen
> after you've disappeared
>
> Timothy Timothy Timothy
> working so hard
> only thinking about
> yourself
>
> Timothy Timothy Timothy
> chained to your desk
> your brain leaking out
> only thinking about
> yourself

> Timothy Timothy Timothy
> already alone
> done with me and Mom
> caring so hard about tests
> he has no more cares to give

I fall asleep.
All my anger in the notebook
instead of
in my head.

When I wake up
the notebook
is gone.

Did I just dream that,
or . . .

Oh, no.
What did I say again?

*

I would like to unzip
my lips
rewind
time
flush that pen
down the biggest toilet
I can find
and suck most of those words
back inside.

*

Timothy leans in the room,
frisbees the notebook
on my bed
and pivots
out again.

When I wanted to go to college
I picked a school close to home
so I could stay here
and take care of YOU.

When I needed a computer
I worked at night
so I could be home in the afternoons
for YOU.

When the bus took too much time
and I needed a car
I sold my record collection
so I could be here
for YOU.

So don't tell me, Levi
don't tell me
you never see me.
I've done EVERYTHING for you
I practically threw away my own life
for YOU.
I've worked for **everything**
and you
you've worked for **nothing**.

His words slice at me
swords
leaving open wounds
that bleed
drips of my heart
but I can't stop reading:

I've held you above my head
since you were born
I've held you
out of the storms
while I've had to fight
to keep us both from drowning.

I've always held you high
Levi
You always came first.

I guess this is what I get
for not teaching you
everyone else matters, too.

My sliced-open heart
just
drips
drips
drips.

And now I'm back home.
Doorbell rings
Tam?
But Mom says no.
Brain rest, the doctor said.
No books.
No screens.
No visitors.
No helping Coach.
No thinking.
No anything.
And since
all my lies
are now lying
around me
like rotten apples
fallen from a tree

I guess
I guess
I really do
have nothing to
do.

Brain rest.
Rest brain.
Brain rest.
Rest brain.
No earbuds.
No music.
No anything.
Just my own thoughts.
My own songs
on repeat
again
and
again
and
again.

*

Except
all of this nothing is
making me think
of everything:

. . . boxing is done
. . . mascot is done
. . . Tam hates me
. . . Dad hates me
. . . Timothy hates me
. . . Mom hates me
. . . now what?

*

Would anyone notice
if I disappeared?
Went away
found a new school?
New friends
New home?

KNOCK

PART II
OUT!

Timothy is right.
I don't know what house arrest
is really like
but
these days
with no boxing
no mascot
just detentions
bus
school
home
I can maybe understand
what it felt like.
I can maybe understand
the itchiness up your spine
when you know you
built this cage
all on your own.

We're all set.
Mom hangs up the phone.

Huh?
I haven't been paying attention
to whatever's going on.

Cincinnati.
Spring break.
Soon.

Oh. Great
I say
as images of oxygen masks
IVs
recovery rooms
flash in front of my eyes.
Something to look forward to.

Boredom punches my guts.
And the holes it leaves
leak out
so many feelings
about how everyone
everyone
is mad at me.
I can't have *everyone* mad at me
so I go to him,
to Timothy's room.
He's at his desk,
says no words
when I walk in

walk right up to his journal
open it
and write:

> *I'm sorry*

while he watches me.

Timothy takes the pen,
he writes:

> **Sometimes words hurt**

I take the pen
and write:

> *I know*
> *I'm sorry*

Timothy writes:

I'm sorry, too.
I would never do anything different
nothing in my whole life.
I would do everything the same
even juvie
everything, Levi
I would do it all again
for you.

I just keep writing:

I'm sorry
I'm sorry
I'm sorry

Timothy takes the pen
wraps his strong arms around me.
I'm sorry.
I'm hiccupping.
I'm crying.
I didn't know
I really didn't know
just how much I've wanted my big brother's arms
to be doing this exact hugging
right now.

✱

Lunch.
Alone.

Tam.
With Kate.
Another table.
Far away.

I put in my earbuds
The Band with No Name
screams in my head.

I wish they had more albums
to get me through
these endless days.

I could ride their words
to a new place
with better lunch,
with zero Kates.

＊

Just a quick Internet search . . .
Who knew?
So many other schools!
Private schools
church schools
home school
unschool.
All these choices,
who knew?

＊

Franklin Middle School:
What do I have here?
Chicken head . . . done
Tam . . . gone
detentions . . . always
so why not a change?
Why not climb
a different tree,
see what I can see?

*

OK, Sport, let's go.
It's Dad time now.

No.

You can't say no.
You're twelve.
Let's go.

NO.
I WON'T.

Annie?
Dad looks to Mom
she looks to me.

He can stay
she says.
He can stay with me.

Pretty sure that's
against the divorce decree
Dad says,
his face turning red.

Levi.
You're coming with me.
Now.

I shake my head.
You gonna pick me up
with your big strong arms,
carry baby Levi
to your car?

My arms are crossed hard
against my pounding chest.

He squeezes his lips
into a very tight line.
Fine
he says,
throwing his hands in the air.
Fine.
See if I care.

✱

After he leaves
he doesn't call.

I don't either.
He doesn't text.
I don't either.
An extralong Dad vacation.
A big fat breather.

We eat together now
more often than not,
just me and Mom.

No more rushing home
late to dinner
because of Chess Club
or "Chess Club"
or
""Chess Club""

So we sit
and we don't say much.
It's quiet
and kind of nice, actually.
Though I admit
I still miss Timothy.

Always studying now,
never out of his room.
Never eating dinner with us,
never watching TV,
never laughing and joking
and teasing me.
I miss him.
I do.

Another thing
in the missing category . . .

BOXING.

I liked it
so much.
So much.
Now that it's gone . . .
I feel lost.

*

It's not just that I want to hit people
or that I like to hit people,
really it's not.
(OK, sometimes it is.)
It's that I like to feel strong.
I like to feel ten feet tall.
And when I am slap dash fast
when I pop and feint
when I dart and jab
I am so fast
I am so strong
I get in my hits
not because I want to hurt someone
but because
it makes me not hurt
anymore.

*

I even miss cleaning the gym,
listening to Coach whistle
while he points at gross stuff for me to do.
Who knew
I'd dream of dirty towels
every night

like
they might wrap up all my problems
and make them go away.

Swoosh

B A M

Swoosh

B A M   B A M

Online videos are my new best friend.
Boxing videos make our living room my gym.
I copy the moves
pause the footwork
watch their faces
as they sweat
concentrate.

And on this one video
I see a kid my age
wearing a shirt that says
Xaviers
and the gym wall also says
Xaviers
and so I pause the video.

I search for
Xaviers
and . . .

Oh.
Whoa.

I feel the hairs on my neck
stand up tall.

Xaviers.

I click and read
click and read
click and read.

It starts in eighth grade!
And goes all the way through high school!
And there's a *boxing team*!
(What!)
And it's a *boarding school*!
((Extra what!))
And it's only a few hours away!
And I want to go!

I really, really want to go.
How did I not know
schools like this
exist?
I want this to be MY school.
I want it to be my school now.

Xaviers.
Sounds like a knockout punch,
a winner supreme.

Of course
there is the small fact
that
ALL TRUST HAS BEEN LOST, LEVI.

So how exactly do I show this to Mom
to Timothy
(to Dad)?

How exactly
might that work?
Hmmm.

*

Speaking of not working,
my puffer has gone kaput.
I mean, it works
but the medicine doesn't.
I feel like my breath
is coming through Mom's coffee straws.
Not all the time,
but more often than not.

I don't want to tell Mom
but I should probably tell her
except I also want to tell her
about Xaviers
and that's not great timing, is it?
She's going to be like
Yes! Awesome! Go to a new school!
Oh wait,
you can't breathe, Levi.
You won't be safe, Levi.
I can't trust you, Levi.
What a dumb idea, Levi.

Ugh.

*

A knock on my door.
You wanna go for a walk?

Timothy.

Don't tell me
you're starting law school now?
And veterinarian school?
And trying out for NASA?

Har. Har.
He sounds serious.
Just come on,
let's talk, OK?

So I say, *OK.*
I know the perfect place.

I don't know why,
but I suddenly
more than anything
want to show him my tree.

*

I wonder if my tree
notices I'm not there.
I wonder if it misses me.
I guess not.
It's just a tree.
But still,
maybe it notices a difference
in its leaves.

*

Timothy looks up into the leaves,
eyebrows high on his forehead.
You climb this thing?
He looks surprised.
It feels weird to see him here
like he's somehow inside
my mind.

It makes me feel
shy

        so

    so

so

I climb.

Levi! What—

My feet hit the bark
and I fly up the trunk
fast
an animal.
I know just how to do it,
just where to place
every step, every grasp.
I don't have to think,
the leaves wrap me up
they say hello
old friend
hello
where have you been?
(I swear
I can tell
they did miss me.)
And Timothy yells up
Levi! Be careful!
And he doesn't know
how full of care
I feel right now
for the world
I'm on top of
again.

*

I don't stay up there very long.
Soon the branches tug,
saying good-bye
as I climb my way down
and smile
at Timothy's surprise.
My arms fling out
when my feet hit the ground,
a magician's trick complete,
a gymnast's final leap.
And Timothy claps.
Wow, he says,
look at you.

You think this is cool?
You should see me box!

We sit in the shade
quietly for a while
drinking sodas
thinking thoughts
then Timothy pulls a different notebook
from his bag.

It's blue, too,
but old, scribbled on
scratched up.
It says *Timothy Davidson*
in fading black letters
on the top.

My journal from when I was your age.
He hands it to me.
You don't have to read it
but,
and now he's the one who looks shy,
you can.
I take the notebook,
a blue time machine
in my hand.

✳

I didn't know any of this!
I flip through the pages.

You stole a wallet?!
Timothy nods.
You stole a car?!
He nods again.

You never told me
you went to juvie
to save my life.
Why did no one tell me that?
You could have told me
I say,
holding the journal.
You didn't have to lie.

We didn't lie.
You just didn't need to know.

But why?

Levi.

Why?

I thought
you would have thought
it was all your fault.
Timothy puts his hand on my shoulder.
But none of it was your fault
that's what I was telling you
by not telling you.

You were a baby.
You were sick.
Now you're better.
Now you're big.
And if I had to,
I'd do it all over
again.

The end.

But is it
the end
now that I've learned
these things?
What else is in this journal?
What else don't I know?

Enchiladas
borracho beans
rice

Mom
Timothy
Me

All of us at the table
for the first time
in a long time
and so what do I do?
Do I say, *Oh, hey*
by the way
I can't breathe anymore?
Or do I say, *Oh hey*
check out this cooler than cool school
called Xaviers.

I mean,
which would YOU choose?

It looks great
Mom says
and I can tell
from her dark sad eyes
there's going to be
a very big
but
and yep
here it is

BUT
BUT
BUT
even if I felt comfortable
sending you off on your own
(which I don't)
we don't have the money
for a school like this
there is no way we could afford it,
Levi.

Don't steal a wallet!
Timothy shouts from the kitchen
while he scoops ice cream

and Mom smiles
for just a second
then goes back to her
sad eyes.
I am so tired
of Mom's sad eyes.

Why do you have to always say no?
I ask
trying not to shout.
Would it hurt to ever say maybe?

To just try that out?
To see how it feels
inside?
To feel the way

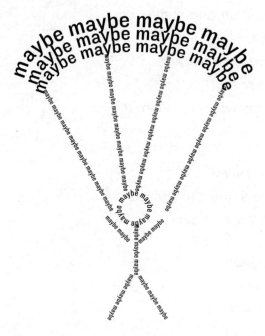

opens like a parachute
instead of closes
like the ground
smashing your face?

Maybes hurt more than Nos
Mom says
almost to herself

and that's when
I stomp
away.

✱

> Do you really want to go away?
> Go to Xaviers?
> What would you do?
> If you got sick?

Timothy and I are sitting on the couch
just writing back and forth now.
How is this easier
than words out of our mouths?
I'm not sure.
But it is.

I
like
to
breathe

Duh

Why
would
I
forget
a
thing
that
could
help
me
breathe
?

Do
you
think
I
am
that
dumb
?

I guess he has no words
for rolling his eyes
because he stares at me,
takes the pen,
rolls his eyes
then writes:

No, Levi.
I think you are the smartest
brightest
kid
I know.
I think you are so smart
you think about so many things
at one time
that sometimes
you forget the most simple
but important things.
I think your brain
is so busy
with smart thoughts
you let the
simple
thoughts
slip by.

That's why
I worry.

This is probably the time
I should mention
the breathing through a straw feeling
but instead
I write back:

> You think I'm smart?
> How smart?

And he snatches the pen
writes:

> Smarter than an elephant.
>
> Shut up
>
> Smarter than an octopus
> escaping
> a tank
> so that it can slip
> down the side
> glide
> across the tile floor

creep
down the drain
and find the ocean
again.

I am
just trying
to find
my own
ocean

After a minute Timothy takes a breath,
puts his hand on my arm
gives a half smile.
writes:

I know.

*

*I just want him to see
what's out there
I want him to see
how things
can be different.*

*How can we trust him
after everything?*

*Maybe everything is a result
of us NOT trusting him.
When have we given him space
to just be . . . him?*

We can't afford different.

We can do anything.

Can we?

*Miracles happen, Mom.
Don't we know that
better than anyone?*

The dishes clatter
as Mom and Timothy
wash and dry
and I hide
a little mouse
around the corner
twitching my ears
listening
listening
listening.

*

All I do now is read
Timothy's old journal.
I can't believe
the things he did.
I can't believe
how much of his time was
spent on . . . me.

*

No wonder Timothy hates Dad.
I never knew all of it . . .
how he just left
with no word,

how Mom and Timothy
struggled so hard.
It was just . . .
so much.
I never knew it was
that bad.

✶

Mom says I can't
just flat-out
stop
seeing Dad
so

I had my vacation from him
but now
here I am . . .

Ta-da.

✶

You can keep boxing, you know.
One concussion shouldn't end
a promising career.

Dad says this
when he picks me up
as if nothing has happened.

And instead of feeling mad,
instead of feeling upset,

it feels like
the first good news
I've ever had
in my whole
dang
life.

But then I remember—
There's no way Mom will say yes,
I sigh.
She's still so mad I lied,
she might never forgive me
ever.

I'll talk to her.
He sounds so confident
it makes me laugh.

Have you ever met Mom?
I ask.

And now Dad laughs.
Just let me talk to her.

✱

I don't really get it,
Dad says,
wiping beer foam
from his beard.

This school
Xaviers
seems a little
tooty-fruity,
doesn't it?
Why do you need
a snooty school,
Sport?
Timothy lived through regular school
and he's a big
strapping
man
now.

Dad sips his beer.
Wipes his beard.

At least
as far as I can tell.

I don't know why
I thought he'd understand.
Sigh.

✳

When I can't breathe like this
it's different
this tightness
in my throat
and I feel my chest contract
feel it act
like a flat
balloon
with its sides stuck together
not filling
just sucking sucking
and it scares me
to feel invisible hands
squeezing my throat

when my lungs
for once
are ready to roll.

*

It's starting to scare me
more
so I finally tell Mom
and of course
she freaks.

*

I don't like these symptoms
Mom says
as I suck my inhaler
and it continues to not work
(stupid inhaler).

I think we should go to Cincy.
Now.

(Now!)

Spring break is practically here,
we'll try to go a week earlier.

She bites her lip.
It means she's worried.
And that makes me worry.
And that makes me
not breathe
even more.

✷

I'm tired of this island at lunch.
I'm tired of missing Tam.
I'm ready to fix it.
I walk up to her table,
everyone stops talking.

Hi.

Tam's face is stone.
She looks right at me.
Hi.

(Kate says a stone-faced *hi*, too.)

I cough. I keep talking.
How are you?

Fine. How are you?

Fine. Well, not so fine.
Looks like we're going to Cincy
for spring break.
Earlier, actually,
to make sure my lungs
aren't about to fall out
or whatever.

Tam's forehead wrinkles
that worried look I know so well
and she starts to say something
but Kate jumps in,

Wow, that sounds awesome.
A road trip
to the hospital?
Looks like you're on some kind of
hospital tour these days.
Way to live it up, Levi.
Way to live life to the fullest.

I almost tell Kate
about all the times
I nearly died
but then I decide

No
she'll just say something dumb
and I'll want to scream
so rather than that
I tell her she's mean.

✳

You think I'm mean?
Kate seems genuinely shocked.
I nod.
Yeah.
I forget I was talking to Tam,
I just
barrel forward
my mouth
a runaway train.
You've stolen Tam
I say.
*I'm like a little fly
you swat away,
and now you think it's funny?
A sick kid in a hospital?
Who's sick now?*
I say.

But. Levi

Tam says, standing tall

arms crossed.

Don't you think you're mean, too?

She glances at Kate,

her lips pressed tight,

and Kate's eyes look from me to the table

before she sighs.

You made fun of her

with that stupid chicken head,

not even trying to be friends,

ignoring HER at lunch every day.

We aren't enemies, Levi.

We aren't enemies, Kate.

We can all be friends.

Can't you two dummies see that?

It's a standoff,

the three of us.

I want to say I already apologized.

I want to say Kate came from nowhere

and now she's everywhere.

I want to say I miss how Tam and I were.

I want to say I miss *her.*

But I can't find any words
so I walk away.

✱

I walk away and
BAM
in my face
signs and flyers
mascot tryouts
coming up.

Every page
every word
stabs me
in the heart.

✱

I want to knock.
I want to go in.
I want to take his journal
or any paper
and ask him
about Tam
about what I should do
but I don't.

His back is to the door
headphones on,
books everywhere.

I'm sure Future Dr. Timothy
will be studying for a while
and for once
I don't want to bother him.
I just stand there for a second
and watch him work so hard.

This is not a yes.
Not a commitment.
Not anything.

Mom stops talking.
Starts over again.

I know this is not exactly a
superfun spring break trip.
So I was thinking . . .

IF Dr. Sawyer says you're fine.
IF he says you're OK,
then maybe

maybe
we can think about Xaviers
maybe.

Mom talks.
Timothy smiles.

So when we're done in Cincinnati
IF everything goes well
we'll swing by Xaviers,
take a short tour.

I start to jump and clap
Mom holds out her hand.

Remember:
It's not a yes.
Not a commitment.
Not anything.
Just a quick visit.
Because it's on the way home.
And I want you to have something . . .
to look forward to.
And your brother wouldn't stop bugging me.
So I said yes
just to get him to leave me alone.

Mom's face is stern.
Serious.
But there's a smile there, too,
so I do three cartwheels
and shadowbox Mom's face.
Timothy walks back to his room
but on the way
he pokes my arm,
he winks.

My insides have exploded
into sparkles.
I'm sure Dr. Sawyer
will be like
Whoa,
this is new
why does Levi's body
have all these sparkles inside?
and that will be because

WE ARE VISITING

XAVIERS

(If he says OK,
which . . .
he will, won't he?
I'll be OK, won't I?)

*

I grab the phone to call Tam
and then I remember
she's still mad
AND she doesn't know
anything
at all
about Xaviers.

*

Tam Tam Tam
my very best,
my only friend.
If I change schools
what would happen
then?

*

I have so many "friends"
but only have
(had?!)
one real friend.
I make people laugh
but does that count
as making friends?
It's something,
the crowd-pleasing,
but it's not everything.
It's not lie on the floor
and talk about secrets
and throw popcorn at each other
and watch movies all night
and visit when you're sick
and finish each other's sentences.

Will I find someone else to do that with?
Do I even want to?

*

I can feel my nerves
tingling in my fingertips
so instead of calling
I'll just walk.
It's kind of far,
but not too far,
and Mom said yes
when I told her

so I'm walking
to Tam's house
to tell her about everything
to see if anything
can ever be
OK
again.

*

How's your face?

Tam stands in the doorway,
looking at me
as she chews her lip.

She mimes Kate's slap.

I had to get a transplant.
Does it look the same?

She rolls her eyes,
smiles,
lets me in.

It looks great.

Then, more seriously
I'm glad you're OK.
I've missed you, Levi.

I've missed you, too, Tam.

✱

My eyes are wide.
In a hole?

It's not a big deal.

Tam, that is so gross.

It's not! It's just how it is!
She laughs, and it sounds
so perfectly perfect
my whole body relaxes.
My whole self smiles.

I could never do that.
I sit on her bed.

Sure you could.

No way.

Then how will you ever camp?

In a cabin. With a real bathroom.

Ha. Well, good luck with that.

Tam's family's big spring break trip is coming up.
They are hiking in some forest
up a mountain
and to a lake
no bathrooms
for seven days.

That makes
Cincinnati
seem like
a piece of cake.

*

Would you really go?
If your mom says yes?

She'll say No
I say that
but don't want to
believe it.

But if she goes crazy
and actually says yes,
would you?

I shrug.
I hate school without you.

I'm there every day.
But her face—
it tells me
she knows what I mean.

I would miss you so much, Tam.
But I already miss you so much.
So.
I look at my hands
feel the bed squish as she sits
next to me.
Her shoulder bumps mine.
I bump hers back.

I told Kate
to be nicer
but she's
jealous of you.

My eyebrows shoot up
sky high.
Jealous of me? Why?!

She's used to being . . .
on top, I guess.
You knocked her down a notch
with that mascot thing.
Plus, she knows how close we are.
She can never be my Levi, you know,
never in a million years.

She's my Kate.
You're my Levi.
I love you
both.

There's a great sweep
of calm
as I lean my head
on Tam's shoulder
and take a deep breath.
Finally,
finally
feeling knocked out
from something good.

Have fun pooping in a hole!
I play punch Tam's arm.
She punches me back.
Harder.
Have fun getting your guts scraped out.

You know that's not what they do,
goof.

Have fun getting your brain transplant, then.
Try not to crack your head,
or get struck by lightning,
or get eaten by a bear.

You're the one getting eaten
by a bear
if you don't poop
in the right hole.

Touché
she says
laughing.
Have a good spring break, Levi.
Take care.

You too, Tam.
You, too.

✳

I know it's silly
to worry
but I worry.
What if something is really wrong with me?
What if Dr. Sawyer says *no way* to Xaviers?
What if something bad is happening inside me?
What if I need a trach again?

*

I try not to think
about all the things
that could be wrong with me
but in my mind I see
the doctor from when my head got bashed
I see her worry
and that worries me.

*

Where's your bag?
I say to Timothy
when I barge into his room
looking for socks
to steal.
Why aren't you packing?

I have to study, Levi,
the MCAT
is so soon.
I have to stay here.

✳

(A question mark formed from the repeated word "WHAT")

✳

How is this going to work?
Timothy is *always* there
when I wake up,
holding a purple popsicle
and a blue sports drink
and sitting next to Mom.

Timothy is *always* there
with a crease between his eyes
but a smile on his face.

How is Timothy not coming?
It has to be killing him
as much as it's killing me.
Right?

I feel dizzy.
I realize
he might *never* come to Cincinnati again.
He'll be at doctor school
if he passes this stupid test
and then Timothy will be gone
poof
and what will I do?

And *that* makes me think of Xaviers
which is, duh,
a *boarding* school
which means I'll be there alone
not just without Tam
but
without anyone.

I grab the notebook off his desk.
I write:

You study so much!

He writes back:

I study because I need to, Levi.
This is my future.
It's right in front of me
the rest of my life
and these books
this knowledge
these are the paving stones
that make up the bridge
to get me to where I want to be.

I take a minute to breathe
because Timothy
can be so dramatic
jeeeeeeeeeez.

How about
the Mississippi River bridge with me?
Or the Ohio River bridge?
And we can say
Hellooooo, Cincinnati
like we always do?

He takes the pen:

I want to!
But I can't, Levi.
Understand?

I slam

the door

because I do understand

but

I don't have to like it.

✶

I'm still working on your mom,
as far as boxing goes.

Dad and me.
One last visit
before the trip.

Oh
I say.
Well
I wasn't holding my
breath.

And then we both laugh
because breathing jokes
yeah
so hilarious.

✶

Have a good trip, Sport.
He says this out the window
of his car
so ready

to drop me off.
Sorry I'm not coming along.

He looks at my shoes
when he says those words
and it's weird because
why would he even say them?
He has never
not once
come to Cincinnati
with us.

Timothy hugs me tight.
You're going to do so fine.
Better than fine.

It's what he always says
before I go to the operating room
but now he's saying it
in his bathrobe
on the front porch.

✳

You'll like it!
No, really!
Mom, just drive.
Trust me.

The Cat Tornadoes blare,
and it's weird
hearing them out loud
not jammed in my ears.

The music expands
rolls around us
blows out the windows like a fog
clearing up the day
crisping up the moment
making us sing so hard,
except the sound from our mouths is drowned out.
The music is too loud, too large.

Mom's mouth has a sideways clench,
her eyes are almost slits
as she drives

as she squints
against
the sun.

I tried handing her sunglasses
she waved them off
I don't like how they dull the colors,
she said,
and it's such a beautiful morning.

So she keeps squinting,
fighting against the glare
saying no to the easy answer
and I think
it's no wonder I'm her son.

We stop a lot
because the road is like a hypnotist
making Mom sleepy
even though I feed
her candy
and Cokes
and jokes.

Timothy usually drives
half the time
and goes too fast
and makes us laugh
and it's weird
without him here.

I wish I could drive
or think of something to say
to keep her awake.

✱

It's like a mother and son vacation
Mom says
in the convenience store
with the floor
covered in sticky spilled
something.

We can do fun stuff while we're there
Mom says.
What about the zoo?
You're not too old for the zoo, are you?

We walk back to the car
and I think of the animals
I used to love
and how now
my heart breaks
because they don't realize
their home
is a cage.
House arrest
for life.

This old place
I feel like we've been here
a hundred times.
Maybe we have.

Dark green carpet
turning light green
where people have walked
from the bathroom
to the bedrooms
to the kitchen
and back.

A hotel
of apartments,
shabby
but fine,
clean but old.

One day
maybe someone will say that about me:
I bet he used to be
really nice.
I bet he used to be
kind of fancy.
Now he's old
but at least
he's clean.

I smile,
give a little wave
to the baby
in the elevator.
His eyes droop—
he looks so tired.
His mom does, too.
I point to my neck,
I had a trach like you.

I kneel down
show him my scar.
He has one hand on a bottle,
he's chewing it, smiling around it.
His other hand touches my scar
then the elevator dings,
our floor.
Mom squeezes the other mom's hand
as we walk out the door,
so many feelings
in one elevator ride.
I wish we could tell them he'll be OK
I wish we could be sure.

✱

We always come to the zoo
if it's 8,846,365 degrees
or if it's too cold to breathe,
we always come here.

The giraffes are my favorite
and I love the polar bears
and the lions, always sleeping
and the penguins
dancing to their own tunes.

The hospital gives us free tickets.
Sometimes we come before
everything.
Sometimes we come after
everything.
Sometimes I eat a pretzel and
run around.
Sometimes I'm too tired and
get wheeled around.
But we
always
come.

So here we are,
but this time
just me and Mom.
It feels a little empty
and unfamiliar
not having Timothy.

✳

This hospital is part of me.
I've been coming here
once
twice
sometimes three times

every year,
forever.

I look out the big windows
so many flags
in a half
circle,
the pickup zone
for when it's time to go home.

I can see the flags bloom
from the waiting room
wind whipping them big
wind whipping them small
my heart also whipping
big and small
as I'm called
down the hall.

✱

No I don't want those socks
to cover my cold toes.

No I don't need a doll
to see where IVs go.

No I don't want a TV
to watch baby shows.

I do need Spaceship Blanket, though
and only Mom knows.

✶

Dad was never gonna come
obviously
I did think maybe he'd call
or text
but he hasn't.

✶

Spaceship Blanket
hidden under my gown
covering my legs,
keeping me safe.

I put a sticker on it,
the one with my name
patient number
birthday
date.
The sticker that's on everything
you want to get back

after surgery
after recovery
when it's time to go home.

I know
they'll find it
hidden under my gown
and when I wake up
it will be by my face
in case
I need it
to calm down.

I'm not so brave
I'm not so old
to not feel happy to see it
when I open my eyes.

They're ready to wheel me out.
I hear a ding,
my phone
in Mom's bag.
I reach in
pull it out
Breathin easy?

a text
from Dad.
I smile
I didn't even know
he knew
we say that.

✳

No text from Timothy.
No call either.
Did he forget the day?
Did he not remember?

✳

Before I open my eyes
I am awake.
My throat hurts bad,
scratched raw
from tubes
and probes.
The room tilts
my stomach flip-flops.
The toughest part of being knocked out?
When you have to wake up.

I try to move my hands
so I can move Spaceship Blanket
in case I barf.

Maybe I moan.
Maybe I'm moving too much.
I feel hands on me
soft voices
Oh look! He's up.

I try to talk
but my throat is too dry.
Levi.
Levi.
Open your eyes.

I push through the fog
wade through the storm
swim up from the bottom
try to surface, re-form.

And then when I make my eyes
open, I feel them go wide
because on the other side
of the bed is Timothy
holding his journal

where he's written in big letters:

SURPRISE !!!

*

How?
is the first word I manage to stammer
as Timothy
hands me
blue juice
and a straw.

I take a sip.
My throat comes alive.
How? I say again.

I bought a plane ticket,
just one way.
I couldn't stand being at home.

*

Dr. Sawyer smiles.
Waking up, Levi?
I nod.
Look at that oxygen level!
He taps the monitor.
It blinks
99 percent.

That,
he says,
is a thing of beauty.
Just like this.

He holds out two photos,
pink circles, gooey and gross.

This is your airway before
and after.
Just had to get my laser
and zap the scar tissue
here
and
here
and
here.

Now you're good as new, Levi.
I could roll a bowling ball
through your throat.

Ouch, I say.

He laughs.
Everything really does look great.

He takes Mom's hand.
I know you were worried,
but this was routine.
No big deal.
After those zaps,
Levi has one of the
biggest
clearest
reconstructed airways
I've ever seen.

He turns to me now,
his smile taking up his whole face.
You've always been such a fighter.
And I hear
you're fighting still
but this time in the ring?

I nod.

And you're thinking of going away to school?

I nod again.
Your mom wanted me to tell you:
I don't see any problem with that.
Either one.
I really don't.
Just keep in touch
for your regular checkups.

He shakes my hand.
I shake his back.
Thank you for letting me be your doctor, Levi.
And good luck, Timothy.
Good luck, Annie.
All my best to you all.

And now

✷

We can still . . . ?
My heart pounds,
hope bubbles up
catches in my
giant throat.
Visit Xaviers
on the way home?

Yes, Levi.
A promise is a promise.

Mom lays her head on my chest
and I can't quite tell
if she's happy
or sad.

✷

And then
we are in a
big
strange
new
Xaviers
world.

＊

Dr. Strong
(for real!
That's her name!)
shakes my hand
and Mom's
and Timothy's, too.
She's the principal person,
the leader of the school.
What a perfect
superhero name she has.
So supercool.

＊

Thank you for setting up this tour.
Timothy is so polite.
Mom says nothing.
I think in her eyes
I see dollar signs
spinning
like in a cartoon.

*

A whole classroom with pedals under the desks
for when your body says go
but your teacher says stay.
The desks don't actually move
but your feet do
they just move and move and move
like they are powering the electricity to your brain
and to your fingers
like you are plugged in
with so much energy
flowing through your wires
that thoughts
fly out
like

sparks sparks sparks sparks
SPARKS SPARKS SPARKS

✻

Students live on campus,
Dr. Strong says,
for the full effect
of the Academy.
If you live nearby
of course you can go home on weekends
and always holidays
and you can get a pass for special occasions.

Timothy's hands are in his pockets.
Mom's eyes are so wide
I think her head
is going to
explode.

Can we see the dorms?
I feel like I am asking to see a king cobra
or a live alligator.
I have never thought of anything more exotic
than living away from home.

*

Small room
two beds
two desks
one sink
big window.
Bathroom
down
the
hall.
One whole room
for a stranger and me.

I don't know what to think.
I can barely imagine . . .
a tiny room as my home?
A roommate I don't even know?
No Timothy watching over me?
No Mom at all?

✱

One last thing . . .
Dr. Strong
(still her name!!)
pushes open two big doors,
we walk into the gym,
and in the corner . . .

It's a boxing ring.

My heart sings
as I run over
grab some headgear
grab some gloves
jump in the ring
before anyone can say a thing
and it feels like coming home
as I jab the air
whoosh my breath
dance my dance
until I sweat
until I realize they're staring
Mom and Timothy
Dr. Strong
and some coach I don't know.

I drop the gloves
take off the headgear
say
Sorry about that
it's just . . . been a while
since I was in the ring.

A big smile spreads across the coach's face.
Dr. Strong nods.
And Mom and Timothy?
Look so surprised that I bet,
I just bet,
I could knock them both out
not with a left hook
but with a sneeze.

✹

I'm not saying I will die
if I don't go to this school
but probably?
I will die.

＊

Before her front door
even opens
all the way
I say:

Did you do it?
Did you poop in a hole?

She nods
very serious,
then says
How about you?
Get your guts scraped out?

I open my mouth
You can see all the way to my tail!

Then I'm inside.
She tells me all about camping
I tell her all about Xaviers
and more about Xaviers
and some more about Xaviers
until she looks like
she might need

to poop in a hole
just to get away from me.

✶

You could come with me.
We'd be a team,
take over the place.

Tam's eyes close slowly
open again.
But I like Franklin.
I'm queen of volleyball.
You know that.

I know that.
I just don't want to leave you.

But Levi,
yes you do.

I want to leave the school.
That's different.
I don't want to leave you.

She nods
OK, yeah.
That's different.

And that's all we say for now.
I guess it's all we need to.

✳

Tam's doorbell rings
right when I'm ready to leave,
so I open the door
watch Kate's smile fade
when she sees me
and not Tam.

It's okay.
I'm leaving.

Levi, wait.

Tam puts her arm over my shoulder,
holding me back.

Kate, come in.

And we stand there
the air
closing in
a net
holding us tight.

I don't want you to fight
Tam says.
Kate, Levi is my Levi.
Right here by my side.

Levi, Kate is my Kate
Right here by my side.

She pulls us both close
so close
I can smell Kate's shampoo.

And we're going to figure it out,
because I need you both
to survive.

Kate and I don't hug.
We don't shake hands.
But somehow her eyes are softer,
and I think mine must be, too.

Tam hugs us both,
and it's a little weird, but
weird
is better than
terrible.

Weird
is a start.

✱

Mom hands me a piece of cake,
a glass of fortified milk-like substance.
OK
she says,
her palms on the table.
IF you get a scholarship,
IF it doesn't cost anything,
you can go to Xaviers.

I nearly drop my fork,
my smile creeping up fast.

BUT,
she says
and I should've known
Mom always has buts
so many buts
a many-butted Mom,

if you go,
she holds up a finger,
IF
you have to come home
every weekend.
You have to come home
if you feel sick.
I've always kept you close,
so close, Levi.
But Timothy helped me understand
that letting you stretch out,
letting you go further
will help you go further.
Does that make sense?
Just . . . no more tricks, Levi.
No more lying.
Ever.
Ever.

Deal! I shout
leaping from the table
hugging her tight.
Deal!
Deal!
Deal!

*

OK
I'm doing it
I'm applying.
It's happening.
Right now.
Just have to start.
I can do it.
Do it.
Do it.
Do it, Levi.
Take what you want.
Make it yours.

*

Are we poor?
I can't really tell.
Do you have to be poor
to get a scholarship?
Do you have to be smart?
What if you are medium poor
and pretty smart?

What if you are pretty poor
and medium smart?
How does it work?
I hope I'm not either
or
especially both.

✳

Who am I?
How will I impact the world?
This is what I have to answer.
These are the only two questions
on the application.
Seems easy
I think.
Uh-oh.

✳

Cursor blink.
I go get a drink.
Cursor still blinks,
brain cannot think.
Cursor STILL blinks.

I start to shrink
away
from the
keyboard.
It seems
so simple
(blank screen cursor blinking).
Who am I?
How will I impact the world?
Ugh. This really stinks
the blank page still there
the cursor still blinks.

✱

Who am I?
I am Levi.
I write.
I am small
but fast
I am smart
but dumb.
And then the words just flow
as I tell the story of my year
up until now.

The words fly from my fingers
as I type
type
type
and I don't know if they're the words
Xaviers will like
but they sound good
to my ears
and look good to my eyes
and my fingers keep going
they just
fly
fly
fly.

✴

And then it's done.
My essay.
My story.
I should ask Timothy to read it.
I should ask him for edits.
I hope it's okay to use his words.
But I don't.
I just hit send,
and away it goes.

And now
in the middle of everything
I'm finally
thirteen.
I asked if I could go sit in my tree
and Mom said yes
so here I am
surrounded by leaves
trying to think.
Thirteen, huh?
What will this year bring?
This past year has been bananas
so this year I'd like bananas
with whipped cream.

bananasbananasbananasbananas
bananasbananasbananasbananas
bananasbananasbananas

✷

A big breath.
One small candle
doesn't have a chance.
Mom smiles
Remember when you used to do that
out of your neck?
She laughs
and we eat cupcakes
and I hug Mom,
surprise her with my squeeze.
Her eyes tear up
and she squeezes back.
My sweet Levi.
You're so big now
it blows
my
mind.

✷

He left before I woke up.
He got home when
I dropped my dinner plate in the sink.
His hair looks like an explosion
circling his head.

His eyes are droopy.
His shoulders are, too.

Hey.

Hey.

Breathing easy?

He shrugs.

Long test?

Words no have mouth fail
he says.
Brain used up.

We smile.
Timothy's MCAT
is over.

✱

He sticks his head out of his doorway
Hey.

Yeah?

Happy birthday, Levi.

I smile.

Happy MCAT day, Timothy.

✳

Three of them
taking turns
with the giant falcon head.
The bleachers like stone
under my butt.
I sit in silence
feeling bad for all my stunts,
wishing I was out there.

Kate is up next
and I know she'll win.
She's way better
than the other two falcons—
their flips and chants
were so lame.

Tam is on the court
off to the side,
she leans in to whisper something
and when she does
she sneaks a kiss
right on Kate's cheek

then Kate is bouncing out onto the court
making everyone laugh and clap
and I wonder
if Tam's little kiss
gave Kate that happy little kick
to her step.

I told you!
I knew I'd come through!
Dad is so proud
you'd think he'd just
conquered the world.

Mom rolls her eyes.
It wasn't you.
I saw him
in the ring
and he was really good.
You should have seen their coach,
the way his eyes
lit up.

Dad puts his hand on his beard
stops talking
just looks at me

then says
too loud
Well, come on!
Let's go!

And we're off to the gym,
boxing once again.

✶

The fact that Dad's words didn't work
and it was my smooth moves
that won Mom over . . .

Hey, Dad, I say,
punching him hard in the arm.
Guess I found a sport, huh?

✶

I'm sure it probably helped
that Dr. Sawyer said I'm OK
more than OK
pretty much
a regular
everyday
kid.

So here I am,
back in the ring,
and oh my gosh
it feels even better
than being back in my tree.

In the ring.

BAM BAM

swoosh

BAMBAMBAM

my video training
paying off.

A few hooks
quick jabs
quicker feints
and boom
I've won the match
in two rounds flat.
That's right, everyone.

Levi
is
BACK.

*

The guys all stare
then they start to clap
Welcome back, Davidson,
Coach says.
Welcome back.

*

Good.
That's all I say when Dad asks how it went.
I try to hide my smile
as I turn and stare out the car window.
I like keeping feelings like this
all to myself
for a little while.

*

There's this job
Dad says
pizza grease on his chin.
It's in Portland.

Oregon?

Yeah. Not a permanent thing.
Just a few months.
Things are feeling tight around here,
you know?
A little too close.
I need to breathe.
You know about that, right, kiddo?
He smiles.

I stare at my pizza,
trying to figure out what he means.
I say
You need to go all the way
to Portland
to breathe?

Think of it like
my Cincinnati.

He laughs.

Something clicks in my brain,
my jaw clenches.
Sadness fills me
so fast.

I lean over
almost nose to nose.
You think things are too close?
What does that even mean?
I'm strangling you?
Making it hard to breathe?
Portland will cure you?
Like Cincinnati cured me?
You need to be cured of family?

This man across the table
who I thought was my dad
sounds like a stranger.

✷

I don't really hear him.
Blah blah Portland.
Blab blah job.
Blah blah more money.

He doesn't seem to notice
he won't be able to drive me to the gym
from Portland.
We won't eat greasy pizza together
in Portland.

We won't have any weekends
in Portland.

He doesn't seem to notice
that what I hear him say is
everything here is strangling him
that my hands are around his neck
and that the real reason he took this job
is to escape
to be alone
to get away
from me.

✱

He's leaving again

I write it on a scrap of paper
push it under Timothy's door.
In one second he's in the hallway
hugging me tight
and I feel like a baby
when I start to cry.

Every day I check the mail.
Every day there's nothing.
Except for today
a long white envelope
with red ink in the corner
Xaviers
Office of Admissions

```
I'm in          I'm in     I'm in I'm in        I'm in I'm in
 I'm in         I'm in     I'm in               I'm in
  I'm in    I'm in         I'm in               I'm in
   I'm in  I'm in          I'm in               I'm in
    I'm in I'm in          I'm in I'm in              I'm in
      I'm in               I'm in                 I'm in
      I'm in               I'm in                        I'm in
      I'm in               I'm in                        I'm in
      I'm in               I'm in I'm in       I'm in I'm in
```

*

They met me,
they read my application,
and they want ME,
Levi,
at their school.

They like Levi
not Timothy
not miracles
not any of the extra stuff
that orbits around me.

They are like the Tam of schools
choosing me
because I'm me
even though they might not know
exactly what they're getting into.

*

I have been awarded a smart kid scholarship
BUT
it's only good for one year
and it doesn't cover the whole cost.
I have to keep my grades up every year

to renew the smart kid award
and no detentions
otherwise Mom has to pay
two kidneys plus Timothy's soul.
So all *A*s and very few *B*s and
I earn MY AWARD
which is:
the privilege of
studying my butt off.

✳

Also I have been awarded poor kid money.
This money is the same every year
as long as we don't suddenly
get rich
out of nowhere.

It isn't a lot of money
but added to the smart kid award
it means some room and board is paid for.

✳

I show the letters to Mom
her hands go to her mouth
Levi!

She squishes me in a hug
lets me go
squishes me again
takes her glasses off her head
slides them to the tip of her nose
and reads the letters again.
Her smile is still there
but it wavers
a rainbow fading in the hot sun.
It's still so much,
she says quietly.
The tuition . . .
We'll have to talk to Dad.
Mom says it like she's chewing sand.
We'll need his help, too.
It's the last thing I want to do,
talk to Dad
but I will
I have to
Xaviers!
It might really be my new school.

✱

It's been so long
it takes a minute
for me to see it
sitting on my chair
so familiar
but missing
for a while now.

I flip it open
and his words are right there:

> You did it!
> I told you!
> You're so smart, Levi!
> Xaviers won't know
> what hit it
> so to speak.

That makes me smile.
I don't even know what to write next.
I just hold the journal
hugging it
to my chest.

★

I just . . .
the world is a hard place, Levi.
We can't always get what we want.
I know you like this school,
but guys like me and you,
we aren't
boarding school guys.

Dad's fries sit untouched.
I sit untouched.

That's the dumbest thing
I've ever heard.
My voice isn't loud
or mean
it's telling the truth.
They want me because I'm smart
because I'm good at boxing
because I am Levi.
And you want me to tell them no
because I'm not a boarding school guy?
Dad.
Just say what you mean.
You don't want to spend the money,
you don't want to help me.

I push away my fries.
I'm done here.
I need some fresh air.
Portland can have you.
See if I care.

✶

That didn't go well
not the way I wanted
Dad is never going to pitch in now.

Even if he does,
Mom will have to pay for some stuff.
Will that be too much
for her?
Am I asking too much
from her?

✶

I'm home now
with Mom
on the couch
quiet.

She already said yes, I won't let her say no.
I'll go find Dad
and pull a yes out of his hairy throat.

*

I'm standing on his porch,
the sun just coming up.
Timothy was asleep when I left,
Mom in the shower.

I knock once
then take the key
from under the mat,
let myself in.

Dad?
He's asleep so
I make myself toast.
I sit at the table.
When the coffeepot comes to life
it smells really good.
I make myself a cup.
Why not?

Levi?
Dad in his underpants

standing in the kitchen.
What are you doing here?

I'm going to Xaviers.
I've made up my mind.
And even with the scholarships
I need uniform money.
What's left of tuition.

You said your new job
pays really well,
so you'll have the money,
right?

I don't understand
why you can't help.
Is it because
you don't want to?

He rubs his hand over his face
Are you drinking coffee?

Dad.
It's your turn to be a man.
I stand.
I hand him the coffee.
I walk out the door.

*

Xaviers called.
Do I have any questions,
they want to know.
Anything they can do to help me out,
they want to know.
They need to know
my answer
by Friday.
That's the one hundred percent
very last day.
It's the last round, Levi.
Time to
      knock
           it
               out.

*

He does not see
the envelope in front of him.
At least he doesn't see it
right away.

He looks up slowly
sweating in the sun
on the porch
putting his book down
on the ground,
standing up
from the rocking chair.

Timothy's hands,
they shake like leaves
in the breeze,
and we go inside,
find Mom.

Read it, he says,
I can't do it.
And Mom takes the envelope,
rips it open,
swallows hard,
holds Timothy's hand.

She says all these numbers
but I don't know what they mean.
My ears are not doctor ears.

Timothy is in a chair now
at the kitchen table
his face buried in his hands
as he listens
his body still
until his hands, fists
move to his ears
when Mom is finished.

She kneels beside him,
and Timothy is crying.
He turns to sob harder
right into her shoulder.
He cries and cries
and I feel a lump in my own throat.
He tried
so hard,
he studied so hard
and now . . .
Mom lifts his head
puts her hands on his wet face.
You did it
she whispers.

Timothy,
this is the first day
so many lives
of so many babies
will be saved.

✳

Dr. Timothy.
It's really happening.
It makes me cry, too
just a little bit
to see him so . . .
happy.
I've never seen him like this.

✳

I've had his journal
this whole time
trying to figure out
what to write
how to respond
after he told me I was smart
after he was so excited
for me to get in to Xaviers.
Now I know.

You are the smart one
Dr. Timothy
You will be the boss
of all those babies
You will save all of them
(you are welcome
for practicing on me)

My brother
the doctor
My brother
the hero

✷

It's late.
The doorbell rings.
Mom looks up from her book.
Who in the world?
I answer the door.

His shirt is wrinkled
so is the check
he puts in my hand.

You're right
he says.
I need to be a man,
but Levi,
you have to understand . . .
I don't have much.
It's not like I have secret accounts
overflowing with cash.

I know, Dad.
I say.
You don't.
But still,
you've gotten off so easy . . .
my whole life.

My chin quivers.
You left us
and somehow
Mom made it work.
She kept me alive,
Timothy too,
and you were gone,
a ghost,
and now you're about
to ghost us again
when we need you.

I get it now.
I get why Timothy runs from you,
why Mom can't look at you.

He doesn't say anything,
just walks away.
The check's in my hand,
and I can't help but wonder
will I ever see him again?

✶

Paperwork signed
dropped in the mail
done.

Xaviers is happening.
I don't know what to think.
It's really happening.
Time to tell Tam.

✶

Get over here
Tam says
and she puts a hand
on each of my cheeks
her palms flat against my face.
What are you doing?
I ask,
my words flat,
squished,
like my cheeks.

It's a face hug!
She laughs.
Because we aren't allowed to real hug
in class.

Congratulations, Levi,
I'm going to miss you so much.

I'll be home on weekends
my squished face says,
and I put my palms against her cheeks
so I can face hug Tam, too.

i want to see you, levi
before i go
i'm sorry, levi
i was a jerk
i will do better

Dad's texts tonight.
Do I believe him
or not?

Are we cool?
Dad's sitting on his front bumper
parked in front of the house.

His eyes look down
his face is soft
he looks like a kid.
Maybe that's the problem.
Maybe *Dad* is the baby.
In all these years *he's* never been a man.

I don't know
I say
and
that's the truth.

I can accept that
he says.
And hey, Levi?
Can you tell Timothy congrats?
I heard he passed his test.
Can I have a hug
before I go?

I give him a fake jab,
a fake right hook,
then I grab
his face

with both my hands
and squeeze
like I'm trying to crack a nut

A face hug
I say.
That's all you get
until you come back
so you better come back.

I will, Levi.
I will, son.

✱

Packing is not fun
especially when you are only allowed
two boxes of things
and one trunk
of clothes.

Tam just throws
stuff in
not paying attention.

Her eyes are a little glazed
so I say

Hey.

And she says

Hey.

And I say

Come with me.

And she says

OK.

And we go to my tree.

✶

We sit quietly
for a long, long time.

I saw you kiss Kate's cheek
I say
to the wind.

Tam's cheek
turns pink.
When?

At the mascot tryouts.
Just before she won.

You made her so happy
she just flew around the court.

Tam nods.
She makes me happy, too.
Her face turns,
her hair blows,
tangles in the leaves.
You make me happy, too, Levi,
just . . . in a different way.
But in my self, my guts, my heart . . .
There's always room for two.

What else can I do?
I stick out my tongue
and say
Kate can have your heart,
I just need your winks.
And maybe one day
for you to teach me
how to poop in a hole.

And that's that.
We hop out of my tree
and go home to finish packing.

And I know
even though
things are different . . .
Tam has my back.

✱

I am not a lumberjack
I am not a cool kid
I am not a chess player
I disappointed a friend
I lied to Mom and Dad
I was mean to Kate
I was mean to Timothy
I felt really bad about it all
I am not a miracle
I am not invincible

BUT

I am smart
I am funny
I am Levi
and I am just so glad
that
I
am
me

*

The drive to Xaviers
goes fast.
Trees,
so many trees
flying by
out the window.

Mom is quiet,
Timothy, too,
and I wonder if their brains
are moving
as swirly fast
flying like butterflies
stinging like bees
so many thoughts
so many worries
so many wonders.

What will you do?
The words come out before
I can catch them.

Huh?
Mom is squinting again

into the sun.
What do you mean?

When I'm at Xaviers and
Timothy is at doctor school . . .
what will you do?
Mom.
What about money?
You're not my giving tree, are you?
You're not going to be a stump without me
are you?

Mom laughs so long
so hard
I think she might choke
then she says
Levi, sweet Levi
I am going to read so many books
and take long baths
and watch TV I want to watch
and eat sushi
and drink too much wine
and Mom just keeps going,
this whole long list.
It sounds like she's been adding to it
for about a hundred years.

*

These same songs I still love,
the noise
the clash
the swirling beats.
But
But
they seem to mean
new things
now
as we drive away from home.

The same songs made new,
just like the same Levi, but new.

I take out an earbud
offer it to Timothy
and we listen together
head to head,
song after song,
the same music as always, and yet . . .
different now.

*

There is a lot of hugging
and Mom cries a lot

and Timothy cries a little.
I try to smile
my throat suddenly full,
a lump
a knot
pushing up
making water leak from my own eyes
and now all the questions
I didn't want to ask
sparring
with my brain.
What will it be like
all by myself?
Who will make me
wash my hands?
What if I get sick?
What if my grades are bad?
What if I smash my head?
How will I make friends?
What if no one likes me?
What will I do then?

I take a puff.
Mom holds me tight.
Levi, Levi,
she whispers in my ear.
Levi.

Everything

everything

is going to be all right.

✱

A box by my bed
has all my stuff
crammed inside
but right on top
I see a blue glint
and I know exactly
what it is.

I open it
find the first empty page
and there are his words:

> Levi, you are MY hero.
> And you always will be.

I run my hands over the page
feel his words pressed into the paper
as I look out the window

a huge tree

right in front of me

blowing

in the breeze

and I say to myself

Hey, Xaviers, Levi is in the house,

and you know what?

I am going to

KNOCK
YOU
OUT

How will I impact the world?
With fast impulses
and dancing feet.
A living Levi
mastering every
strategy.

A man's man
ladies' man
man about town.
Causing knockout
after knockout,
winning round
after round.